SER

The Seventh Da,

By Leslie Swartz

MW01139695

Copyright 2019, Leslie Swartz

Library of Congress Control Number: 2020903741

ISBN: 9781097632800

The devil can cite Scripture for his purpose.

William Shakespeare

Prologue

"Another one?" Lilith implored as Allydia emerged from the entrance of a chamber well hidden in the panels along the temple's far left wall, the stain of crimson still visible on her lips and chin.

"It was like being stabbed frantically with a stitching awl," Allydia complained.

Lilith giggled as she poured her step-daughter some wine. She admired the engravings on the gold cup as she handed it off and sat on her throne. The limestone was cool against her bronze skin which she had lovingly draped in a sheer, fringed shawl.

"Allydia, dearest," she condescended. "How many times must I explain that you have to *train* a man to please you? No man will ever seem worthy of you if you do not teach him to be."

"I refuse to put that kind of effort into a relationship I expect to last only until sunrise," Allydia retorted as she sat in her own throne, somewhat smaller and to the left of her step-mother's. "If a man can not satisfy me, he will be my dinner."

"You will never be satisfied. What you are disallows it," Lilith told her. "But, at least you'll be well-fed." They raised their cups to each other and drank.

"Mmmfff," the man sitting at Lilith's feet whined. She kicked him in the ribs before reprimanding him.

"I will give back your speech when I'm sure you've learned your lesson!" The naked man cowered and nodded, his lips still fused together. Several other servants stood around the throne room doing their best to remain still and silent, awaiting instruction, beratement, or torture. They only wished that the hoards of worshipers that gathered around the temple day and night would one day rise up against these creatures and save them from their servitude. They knew, however, that that was a hopeless fantasy, so they suffered, resigned to their fate.

"I'm bored," Lilith lamented. "I think it's time for us to move on. Spread out. Expand our empire."

"What did you have in mind?" Allydia wondered.

"I'm so glad you asked," Lilith said giddily. "I have great plans for us. Our army is set to invade all of the nearby cities, all at once! They only await my order. Nippur, Nineveh, Assur. Once I've taken control there, I can take what's rightfully ours."

"Babylon," Allydia concluded.

"Yes! *We* reign here, not them. We'll take the city and I will find a way to close the Gate, *permanently*. With that done, the entire world can be ours. It's so much bigger than you know. I can't wait to show you."

"My Queen," a man said from across the room. He had entered while the two were talking and didn't want to be punished for interrupting but this couldn't wait.

"Yes," Lilith said quizzically.

"I want to thank you for the honor of your presence and I've come today to ask that you please save my farm. My crops are dying," the man explained. "I have four children at home that won't survive if I can not feed them."

"If you were me," Lilith asked. "Would *you* care about that?"

"I've not come empty-handed, my Queen. I offer sacrifice." He unwrapped the bundle he'd been carrying to reveal a sleeping infant. Lilith's interest was piqued. She sniffed the air.

"Well, that baby is brand new," she said lustfully.

"Yes," he confirmed. "Born last night. I have no way to feed her. She is yours if you help me. I beseech you."

"Where is that child's mother?" Allydia asked.

"Dead," he told her. "The delivery proved to be too difficult."

"Dead?" Lilith queried. "It's not much of a sacrifice to offer a burden."

"Please, my Queen. I will give you anything. Take of me what you will."

"Fine," Lilith sighed. "I'm feeling generous. I accept your sacrifice."

"Thank you!" the man gushed, laying the baby at Lilith's feet, the mute servant staring in horror. "Thank you so much." He placed his hand over his heart and bowed as he left the temple, relief washing over him like rain.

"Why do they think I can solve their problems?" Lilith asked.

"They think you're God," Allydia reminded her.

"Oh, right," she chuckled.

Lilith bent down to retrieve the quiet bundle but before her hands could reach, the servant snatched the child up and ran.

"Is this a joke?" Lilith wondered. She flicked her wrist, snapping the man's neck from across the room. He fell to the floor, taking the child with him. She started to cry.

Just then, the Earth began to tremble. Wind blew in from the small entrance. They could hear the screams of people outside as the mud bricks of the building started to crumble. One of the servants, a woman whose own child was recently taken by her mistress, never to be seen again, took the opportunity to grab the wailing infant and flee. Suddenly, the shaking stopped and as the dust settled, they could see a figure standing before them.

"Sister," the man said slyly.

"It can't be," Lilith said, stunned. "I thought you were in, what did He call it?"

"Hell," he affirmed. "I was. I will be again. But I won't be going alone."

"You wish to imprison me, brother?" she guffawed. "On what grounds?"

"Well, there's a list, isn't there?" he jeered. "Crimes against humanity covers most of it. You know how He feels about His people. But, He's been willing to overlook that until now. Bigger problems to solve. But going after The Gate? Too far."

"I haven't done that yet," she challenged.

"But you would if left to your own devices. You forget He sees all. Nice to see you again," he said, turning his attention to Allydia.

"Don't know that I can say the same," she responded.

"Don't worry," he comforted. "I'm not here for you."

Lilith rolled her eyes. "I'm bored again," she huffed. "You, dear brother, have overstayed your welcome. Shoo." She waved her hand, sending him flying into the far wall, cracking it further.

"I was hoping to do this gently but you give me no choice." He opened his arms and waved his hands toward himself. The remaining servants all came forward, shock and horror covering their faces as they were forced to move closer and closer to their Queen. For the first time in her very long life, Allydia saw fear in her step-mother's eyes. The servants now rushed to Lilith, grabbing her and holding her steady. She fought them, tossing their bodies around like pillows. But they kept coming. Even the ones she killed reanimated and came for her. They forced her down into her throne and held her there as her brother neared.

"No!" she barked. "You can't!"

Allydia backed away, knowing what the man was capable of.

Lilith's anger turned to fear as her fate seemed sealed. "Please, brother," she begged. "We can all rule this world together. You don't always have to do what He says!"

"You know that simply isn't true," he said, kneeling before her and placing his hand on her head. He began the incantation while she screamed.

"Stop!" she pleaded. "Don't! Please! LUCIFER!"

Chapter 1

"How have I been since our last session?" Wyatt said impatiently, shifting a little in his seat. "Well, let's take stock. My wife left me because I'm not father material and I lost my job because, apparently, I'm too crazy to run into burning buildings. All in all, I'd say the last week hasn't been exactly stellar."

The therapist raised his eyebrows and took off his glasses. He sat them gently on the table next to him and picked up a pen. He scribbled something down and turned his gaze back to his patient.

"I'm very sorry to hear that, Mr. Sinclair. Truly," he told the man, who was visibly becoming more and more uncomfortable.

"Thanks," Wyatt said flatly.

"What would you like to discuss first?" the doctor asked, keeping his voice calm and soothing, almost monotone. His timbre seemed to annoy Wyatt more, but the doctor was steady, knowing that what this patient needed at that moment was a cool sounding board. That and a shit ton of antipsychotics.

"Work, I guess," Wyatt said halfheartedly. He was tired, not having slept in about thirty hours. Between that and days of weeping, his eyes were pained and bloodshot, barely able to stay open. Getting fired had pissed him off but losing his wife destroyed him. He would have to work his way up to talking about her.

"All right. Tell me what happened," the doctor instructed, readying his pen for what he was sure would be a lot of note-taking.

"It was the hallucinations," Wyatt confessed, brushing his dark hair away from his right eye. "They're not going away, no matter how many drugs you put me on."

"Are you not seeing any improvement?" the doctor asked.

"No," Wyatt answered, clearly upset. "I was *convinced* a woman was screaming for help inside an apartment next to one we'd just put out. I was so sure, I took an ax to the door. The eighty-seven-year-old man that lives there, who was the only person inside at the time, almost had a heart attack. He's suing the department."

Hallucinations continue. Need to up dosage of Risperidone, the doctor wrote. "And how does that make y--"

"I swear to God if you ask me how getting fired makes me *feel*, I'm leaving right now," Wyatt threatened. He slicked his hair back out of his face and took a deep breath. "I understand why they let me go. I don't blame them," he asserted. "I'm just sick and fucking tired of seeing and hearing things that aren't there." He again combed his hair back, trying and failing to keep it out of his eyes. He knew he was long overdue for a haircut, but he just couldn't muster the energy to care. He couldn't remember the last time he'd shaved. Probably four days ago, maybe five. Today was the first time he'd showered in that same amount of time. What was the point? Without Annie, life didn't seem worth living and the mundane routines of maintaining that life felt like a profound waste of time.

"I hadn't even told her," Wyatt admitted. "I was looking for another job, hoping I could just say I needed a change. Like it was *my decision* instead of having to tell my wife that I was put out on my ass for being a lunatic."

"Let's talk about Annie," the doctor insisted. "Clearly, that's what's bothering you the most." His voice was unconvincingly sympathetic and Wyatt struggled not to let his anger at the doctor's lack of sincerity ruin the session. Over the years, Wyatt had had many psychiatrists, none of which had been much help. While the hallucinations persisted, Dr. Stratford had been the only one to help him get through some of his more common issues like his mother's death, his father's distance and cruelty, and his general feeling of not belonging. The truth was, he was good at his job whether he actually cared about Wyatt's well-being or not.

"Sure," the patient started, taking a deep breath and letting it out slowly before he began. "I'd spent all day putting in applications at random places; gas stations, stores, restaurants. *Anything* to bring some money in while I figured out what my next move should be. Do I work at my father's firm like he'd always wanted? That sounded like being in Hell, but as long as going back to school and becoming a stripper were on the table, I couldn't rule anything out. But, on the way home I decided that I wanted to train to be an EMT, something where I'd still be helping people. Then, I remembered they don't allow people with severe mental illness to do that job so by the time I walked in the door, I was pretty messed up already." The aggravation on his face turned to sorrow as he thought about his wife and what he'd seen when he entered the apartment that day. Tears began to swell in his eyes. And here he was, thinking he had no tears left in him. He did his best to settle the anger that had again built up in his chest before continuing. "I got home and she was gone. Her clothes, her books, her computer. The art from the walls, most of the dishes. Her stupid cartoon character pillow that I made fun of her for keeping even though it was old and dusty and smelled bad. All gone. She left a note. Who does that? Sixteen years together and she writes a *note* after leaving the place looking like the scene of a robbery." He sighed heavily as his anger once again turned to sadness. "I must have read it ten times."

"Would you like to tell me what it said?" Dr. Stratford asked.

"No, not really but I will," Wyatt told him, pulling the letter from his back pocket. "I expected you might want to hear it," he said as he unfolded the paper. He cleared his throat and began to read.

"*Wyatt,*

I want to start by saying that I never thought I'd do this. You know I love you. Like, more than life. But your behavior gets more erratic every day. I watched you pull your hair out in a fit because 'the woman's voice' wouldn't be quiet. Your night terrors keep me awake because I'm afraid you'll hit me in your sleep. The final straw was when you broke the bathroom mirror in a rage fit because you didn't recognize your own reflection. You're on I don't know how many pills and none of them seem to be working and the worst part is how helpless I feel. I want to be able to make things better for you but I'm about as worthless as your prescriptions. The thing is, I want to have children. You know that. You must also know the reason why we've never tried to have any. Besides our kids potentially inheriting your disease, I just don't trust that you'd be a safe person for a child to be around. I know that you'd never hurt me or a kid on purpose but you have to admit, you're dangerous. It's not your fault and I'm not angry with you. You're a good person and you deserve to have a normal life, which is why I think a stay at a treatment center is something you should consider. I don't have the heart to commit you against your will, but I'm begging you to get the help you need. Sadly, I don't think you will so I have to think about my future. If I'm ever going to become a mother, I have to move on. I'm so sorry. -- Annie"

He wiped the tears from his face and put the letter back in his pocket. As he gathered himself, he noticed that the doctor, too, had gotten misty.

"You old softy," Wyatt teased.

The doctor gave a quiet laugh. "I'm sorry," he said, dabbing his eyes with a tissue before offering one to his patient. "That's inappropriate. I should be stoic and objective. But, I know how hard you've been working and what you've been through to make the progress you have. No matter how unflappable I should be here, that letter was a punch to the gut."

Wyatt was shocked. He'd never seen the doctor get emotional. He honestly didn't think he cared that much. He watched as the therapist wrote something on a prescription pad, set it aside, and put his glasses back on.

"I'm not sure what 'progress' you're talking about," Wyatt said.

"Well, you're here, aren't you?" the doctor pointed out. "The Wyatt Sinclair I met two years ago would still be in a heap on the floor if his wife left him. Or worse. But, instead of wallowing or hurting yourself, you came here to talk. That's progress."

"If you say so."

"I do," Dr. Stratford confirmed. "Now, how do you feel about your wife suggesting inpatient treatment? Had you discussed that with her before?"

"A couple of times," Wyatt told him. "My dad locked me up in one of those places when I was in college. Senior year for three months. I almost didn't graduate because of it. I think the only reason I got into law school was that he paid someone off."

"Yes," the doctor said. "I have the records from your time at Clear View. The doctors there marked your diagnosis as 'unchanged' when you left."

"Yeah, the place was useless," Wyatt stated. "That's why I told Annie I'd never go back."

"How do you feel now?" the therapist inquired. "Do *you* think you need hospitalization?"

He thought for a moment, admitting to himself that a stay in the loony bin probably wouldn't hurt. It at least couldn't make things any worse than they were now. But, he also had very little faith that one of those places could do him any real good.

"I honestly don't know," he conceded. "I know I need *something*, that's for goddamn sure."

"Let's put a pin in it for now," the therapist suggested. "The nightmares. Are you able to remember anything more about them?"

"Not really," Wyatt said. "It's just the same old thing. People getting hurt, needing help and me saving them, somehow."

"But, you don't know how."

"No."

"And you still can't understand what the people in the dreams are saying to you?"

"No. It sounds like they're speaking Latin or Greek or something."

"But, you know they need your help?"

"Yeah, they're bleeding and screaming and crying. It's chaos all around. Like a war zone," Wyatt remembered.

"But, you save them."

"Yes."

"Every time?"

"Yes."

"And it's important to you that you save people in your real life? Not just help them but save their lives?"

Wyatt hadn't made the distinction before but if he was being honest with himself, he supposed he *did* love the feeling he got when he saved someone from certain death. Seeing the joy, relief, and gratitude on the face of a person who, not a minute before, was sure they were about to die was maybe the only thing in Wyatt's life that gave him any real sense of happiness.

"I guess so," Wyatt confessed.

"Interesting," the doctor said, writing again in his notebook. "Tell me about the woman's voice. Is it still repeating the same question?"

"At least twice a day. But, lately, it's getting more, I don't know, annoyed. Like it's mad that I'm not talking back."

"So," the therapist asked, looking up from his paper and into Wyatt's eyes. "It wants to know, 'where are you?' Does it mean emotionally? Where you're at in your treatment? Is it asking if you think you're getting any better? Worse?"

"I have no idea."

"And you ignore it."

"Yes."

"And you think ignoring the voice is angering it?"

"I really couldn't tell you, doc. It's definitely pissed off about *something*. The last week, it's been so loud, I can't hear anything around me. It's like I'm on the truck with my ear pressed against the siren. It's getting to be unbearable."

The doctor sat quietly for a moment, tapping his pen on the rings of the notebook. After some thought, he leaned forward and looked Wyatt dead in the face.

"Next time it happens," he told the patient. "Answer it."

Wyatt's eyes grew wide. The doctor's advice was the opposite of everything he'd ever been told about how to deal with his hallucinations.

"Answer it?" he questioned. "That's not at all what any of you shrinks have ever told me to do. Wouldn't that make it *worse*?"

The doctor shrugged. "It could. Or not. The thing you have to remember about the voices in your head is that they're *you*. They're a manifestation of some part of your subconscious, as intrusive and bewildering to you as they may be. Maybe telling the voice what it wants to know, i. e., admitting to yourself where you believe you are emotionally and psychologically, is the first step to real improvement. I have to be honest with you, Wyatt, I'm increasing the dosage of your antipsychotics and mood stabilizers but I don't have high hopes of them being magic bullets. While you've learned how to cope with some of the deep-seated issues stemming from your childhood, you've made very little, if any progress in managing the symptoms of your schizophrenia. I want you to take these." He handed Wyatt the prescriptions. "Come back in three days and let me know if they're working any better. We'll go from there but if you're still having episodes that you can't control, like not recognizing yourself in the mirror, after a month of the new dosages, we may have to consider other options."

"Other options," Wyatt stated. "Like Clear View."

"I wouldn't recommend that particular facility but yes, somewhere like it."

"For the record, doc, I hope it doesn't come to that," Wyatt said, standing up to leave and reaching out to shake the doctor's hand.

"Neither do I, Mr. Sinclair." He took his patient's hand, jumping back a little at the static shock he felt.

"Sorry," Wyatt said.

The doctor smiled. "You'd think I'd be used to it by now. See you in a few days." He patted him on the shoulder and watched him leave. He could see him through the window of the small brick office as he got into his car and drove off. He genuinely felt bad for Wyatt Sinclair. Most of his patients

were easily treated with antidepressants or antianxiety
medication. But, Wyatt was the real deal. He needed real help
that the doctor was worried he wasn't capable of providing.
Recommending inpatient treatment was the last thing he
wanted to do but he feared that, in this case, it might be the
only viable option.

Wyatt was anxious to start his new prescriptions.
Luckily for him, the pharmacy was just a few blocks away
from the therapist's office. As he stood at the counter waiting
impatiently for his scripts to be filled, he noticed how empty
the store felt. There were a couple of employees milling
around but otherwise, the building was quiet. He took his
phone from his back pocket, hoping for a text or missed call
from Annie but unsurprisingly, there was nothing. He sighed
a little as he returned the phone and let his eyes wander, first
to the pharmacist and then to the bottles and boxes on the
shelves behind her.

Prepopik. Suprep. Moviprep. As he read, he was
somewhat amused by just how bored he had to be that he was
occupying himself by examining colonoscopy preparation kits
from twelve feet away.

"It'll just be a few more minutes, sir," the pharmacist
told him from behind the counter.

"Thank you," he replied.

Where are you? he suddenly heard. He looked around,
hoping that it was the pharmacist speaking to him again. But,
he knew better. It was 'her', the voice in his head. It sounded
testy and Wyatt grew nervous. First of all, he wasn't stoked
about the idea of losing it in public. Secondly, the doctor had
told him that the next time the voice asked the question, he
should answer it but was that smart? Would that give it more
power over his mind? Make it more real?

Wyatt was startled by the sound of the door opening to
three men arguing about how much beer they needed for the
night's festivities. They were throwing a 'rager' and needed
enough for everyone to get 'lit' and still have enough money

to get tacos later. Wyatt rolled his eyes at how immature they seemed and how petty their problems, or even possibly their entire lives, must be. He remembered his own college days, getting wasted most nights, his friends thinking he was the life of the party. In reality, he had been trying, unsuccessfully, to drown out the noise of people that weren't there.

"Here you are, sir," the pharmacist said, handing him the bag containing his medication. "You have a good day."

"Thanks, you too," he said, unable to return her bright smile.

Where are you?! the voice insisted, louder and sounding more frustrated than before. Wyatt left the store quickly and fumbled with his keys as he crossed the parking lot. *Tell me where the fuck you are,* the voice demanded. *I'm sick of this shit.* It was angry now, the angriest he'd ever heard it. It was so loud, it completely drowned out the noise of the busy street in front of him. He made it to his car and tried to get the key in the door but his hands were shaking too violently. He looked around. The parking lot was empty aside from a few uninhabited cars and a truck he assumed belonged to the frat guys inside based on how badly it was parked. This was it, he decided. He would answer the voice as the doctor had suggested. He had to. Nothing could be as bad as how he felt right now.

"I'm a wreck!" he admitted. "I'm completely fucked up and I have no idea how to get better. As far as I can tell, there's not a way. You want to know where I am?! I'm at the corner of Miserable Avenue and Mad as a Hatter Boulevard!"

What the fuck? The voice asked. *Listen, we don't have time for you to have a meltdown right now. Tell me where you are, physically. I need a location so I can come get you. Freak.*

Wyatt dropped his keys. He was having a full conversation with a voice in his head and, not only that, it wanted to 'come get him'. Did he have multiple personalities on top of everything else? What was going on? He could barely breathe. He reached into the bag and retrieved one of the pill bottles but he was trembling so hard, he couldn't get it opened.

WHERE ARE YOU?! TELL ME WHERE YOU ARE! The volume of it was painful. It boomed in his head with such resonance, he thought he might have a stroke. He squeezed his eyes shut and put his hands to his head. His heart was racing and he couldn't think straight. What was happening?!
TELL ME!

"I'm at a pharmacy on Nine in Howell!" he yelled and as he did, a lightning bolt hit a lamppost, spewing sparks and filling the air with thunder and blinding white light. Wyatt fell to the ground, shaking, trying to catch his breath. His heart was pounding in his ears but that was all he heard. The voice was gone. The parking lot was silent.

He picked up the medicine and got in his car, finally able to unlock the door. He hurriedly opened the bottles, taking a pill from each one and dry swallowing them. He sat there, breathing heavily, trying to collect himself. Through his mirror he could see the frat guys leave the store, piling several cases of light beer in the bed of their truck before taking off. *At least no one saw me freak out,* he thought.

As he calmed down, he watched car after car speed by. The traffic reminded him of when he had moved there; of *why* he had moved there. Annie's mother lived in Howell and after graduation, she wanted to move back there to be close to her. So, they packed up their studio apartment and left the city. Manhattan had always been Wyatt's home but after law school, what did he have to stay for? He wasn't interested in becoming a lawyer as his father had always insisted. What he wanted was to save lives, so he bulked up and became a firefighter. His father was enraged. He remembered thinking that he'd never seen John so furious. After that, their relationship was strained, to say the least. They hadn't spoken since not long after the wedding; almost ten years. Wyatt wondered what his father would say when he found out that Annie had left him. He wondered how he was, if he was in good health. After all, he *was* getting older. Mostly, he wondered if he had forgiven him for leaving or come to terms with his son being 'different'. He sighed heavily. He was more relaxed but still a little shaken. He decided to go home, take some Xanax, and go to bed.

Three days had gone by and he hadn't heard the voice once. It was gone, just like that, and all he had to do was tell it what it wanted to know. It felt insane. He'd always thought he should never do what 'the voices' told him to. That that was how you end up becoming a mass shooter or a man that dresses like his dead mother and hoards cats. But, it worked. The voice was gone and Wyatt was starting to feel like he might be making some progress. For once, he was excited to see his therapist. He was feeling hopeful and as he sat down on the brown leather sofa in the doctor's office, Dr. Stratford could see the change in him. He looked healthier, stronger, and more relaxed than usual. He couldn't believe it. The new dosages must have done the job.

"Mr. Sinclair," the doctor began. "You look, dare I say, almost happy."

"Let's not get ahead of ourselves," he said. "But, I think I'm doing a little better."

"Tell me what's going on."

"A miracle, I think," Wyatt joked. "After I left here a few days ago, I heard the woman's voice again. I told it where I was, just like it wanted. I immediately started taking the new pills and I also took a Xanax that night." He sat back, feeling more comfortable there than he ever had. "I haven't heard the voice since."

The doctor looked at him with amazement. "Really?" he asked. "That's incredible. And what about your other symptoms? Hallucinations? Nightmares?"

"Still there," Wyatt told him. "But, if I can get rid of the voice, maybe I can eventually get rid of all of them."

"So, what your subconscious wanted was for you to address your own emotions after all," the doctor stated, proud that he had been able to finally help his patient have a breakthrough.

"No," Wyatt said. "It wanted me to tell it where I was. Like, the cross streets or something."

The doctor was baffled. "What?" he wondered. "It just wanted to know your physical location?"

"Yeah."

"And it gave you no more information? Why do you think that is?"

"Because," a woman explained as she burst through the office door. "I should really tell him what he needs to know in person." She sat next to Wyatt on the couch, a mischievous grin lighting up her face. She was beautiful with big brown eyes, high cheekbones, and dark hair.

"Excuse me, who are you?" the doctor asked sharply.

"Name's Taran Murphy but I don't really go by that. My parents were Irish but I feel like it's a little unfair to claim an ethnicity when I'm not really from here, you know?" She looked at Wyatt and smiled. "You can call me Gabriel."

He felt sick. Her voice. It was the woman's voice in his head. The incessant yelling, asking where he was nearly every day since he was eighteen. It was her, he was sure of it.

"You can see her?" he questioned the therapist.

"Of course," he answered matter-of-factly. "We are in session, Miss. You need to leave."

She leaned forward to more directly look at the doctor. "What are his issues, doc?" she taunted. "Let me guess. Sees things no one else can see. Hears things no one else can hear. Bad dreams. Maybe an issue with electricity, like, static shocks? Maybe," She looked back at Wyatt who had gone pale and felt like his heart would explode in his chest. "Lightning?"

"How do you know that?" Wyatt breathed. He had been convinced that the lightning in the parking lot was just another hallucination.

"I know everything," she replied nonchalantly. "For instance," She looked back at the doctor. "You were meant to be a concert pianist, but you never thought you were good enough, so you do this instead. All the joy you could have brought to people's lives, all that God-given talent, wasted. But, hey, a lot more stability in medicating the crazies, am I right?"

The doctor was stunned. "How could you possibly..."

"Did you not hear me when I *just* said I know everything?" She stood up, grabbing Wyatt's hand and pulling him up with the strength of a linebacker. "Come on, B, we gotta bounce."

She dragged him through the lobby and out to the parking lot like he weighed nothing. As the shock wore off, Wyatt, with much effort, yanked his hand away and stopped.

"Who are you?" he asked, not quite believing this person was made of flesh and blood and not just a figment of his imagination. "What do you want?"

"Short answer," she responded. "I'm your sister...kinda. We'll discuss it later. Right now, what I *want* is for you to call your dad *before* he calls you. It'll make him feel like you give a shit and he'll be less of a dick when you go see him. I'll meet up with you when you're done." She got into a tiny black sports car that Wyatt guessed cost more than what he made in two years at the department and looked up at him through the still opened door. "Listen, I get it," she told him. "You thought you were out of your mind so you ignored me. I'll get over it eventually but as of now, I haven't forgiven you for making me schlep out to Jersey so you owe me." She took the sunglasses from her dashboard and put them on. "Call your dad." With that, she slammed the car door shut and peeled out like a stunt driver.

Wyatt stood there, motionless, not sure what to do next. Behind him, he could hear the quick footsteps of someone approaching. He turned to see Dr. Stratford hurrying toward him.

"Are you all right?" the doctor asked.

"I'm fine," he lied.

"Who was that woman?"

"I don't have a clue," Wyatt told his doctor. "But, you could see her? She wasn't in my head?"

"I can assure you, she was very real. I have half a mind to call the police and report her as a stalker."

"You think she's a stalker?"

"It's the only thing that makes sense," the doctor surmised. "How else could she know about my past?"

How else indeed? A stalker. That was the only rational explanation. But, what about her voice? It was too curious of a coincidence for Wyatt to ignore.

"I'm going to have to reschedule our appointment if you don't mind," he told the doctor. "I need to handle some things."

"Of course. Just set it up with Marjorie."

The men nodded goodbye to one another as Wyatt headed toward his car. He sat in the driver's side seat and closed the door, looking at himself in the mirror.

"What the fuck?" he whispered to himself. "Okay, let's think about this logically. The receptionist saw her. Stratford saw *and* talked to her and confirmed she's a real person. Whoever that was is real, not a hallucination. So, she *can't* be the voice in my head." But, he was sure that the voices matched. He knew it in his bones. "But, how did she know about the lightning?" he asked himself. "How did she know about the dreams and the doctor? How--" he stopped, suddenly realizing what he was doing. "And I'm talking to myself. Awesome." He shook his head and turned the key in the ignition.

His head was swimming with thoughts as he drove home. Who was the woman, really? How was she connected to the voice in his head, if she was at all? Was he just projecting? And did she say she was his *sister*? Did his father have another kid he didn't know about? It was possible, he guessed. His mother had been dead for decades, and while he had never seen his father date, it was entirely in the realm of possibility that he just kept his girlfriends hidden from his son. As a child, Wyatt's father had all but worshiped his dead wife's memory. There were pictures of her everywhere, though he never spoke about her. To this day, Wyatt still had no idea how she died. All he was ever told was that she had died when he was a baby. He had always assumed it must have been during childbirth by the distance his father put between them his whole life. But, who knows? Could have been a car crash, suicide, rogue meteorite. Anything was possible.

At his apartment, Wyatt sat at his kitchen table, spinning his cell phone on the black lacquered wood as he procrastinated. He took note of the takeout bags that had piled up on the counters and the dishes that sat unwashed in the sink. Since his wife left, he'd really let the place go to shit. He could picture Annie at the sink, hands covered in suds, laughing while she scolded him about the mess. *We'll get ants,* she would have said. He'd just smile in agreement and throw the garbage in trash bags, tie them up, then kiss her cheek before taking them out to the community dumpster. Later, they'd have dinner and talk about their days, make weekend plans, and watch television before heading to bed where they'd have boring but satisfying sex, read a little, and go to sleep. *Get it together,* Wyatt thought, rubbing his eyes as he brought himself back to reality.

He took the phone in his hand and pulled up his father's number. He *had* been thinking about his dad recently and had wanted to reach out but it never seemed like the right time. Maybe the woman *was* a stalker, nothing more. Either way, it probably *was* a good idea to check in with his dad, if for no other reason than to rip off the band-aid of telling him about Annie.

"Let's get it over with," he said to himself as he hit the call button.

"Hello?" John answered, not recognizing the number. He rifled through some papers on his desk while he waited for a reply.

"Hey, Dad," Wyatt choked out, trying not to sound nervous. "How are you?"

John raised his eyebrows in surprise and sat slowly in his chair. "I'm all right," he responded coldly. "And you?"

He wasn't sure how to answer the question, so he settled on honestly. "Weird." He laughed a little as he said it.

"Well, that's not really news, is it?" John said. "How are things? How's Annie?"

"She left," Wyatt told him. "She wants kids and thinks I'm unfit. She's not wrong."

"I'm sorry to hear that," John said, almost dismissively. "Listen, I was just about to call you. There are some things we need to go over. When do you think you could make some time to come home?"

Home. The word sounded strange coming out of his father's mouth. The woman *did* say he would go see his dad and the truth was, he missed New York terribly. The pizza alone was enough to justify the trip.

"Whenever you want," Wyatt said. "I've got some time off."

"Great. Later today work for you? I've got some paperwork to finish up but I'll be done in a couple of hours."

"Sure. See you then."

"See you then," John hung up and continued going over his files.

Wyatt put the phone down and sighed heavily, relieved the call had ended but more confused than before he'd made it. The woman had been spot on about everything she'd said. His father *would* have called him if he hadn't called first and he *was* going to see him. If she was a stalker, she was incredibly thorough.

Chapter 2

Wyatt stood at the massive entry of his childhood home. The building that had been erected in eighteen eighty-four was as beautiful as ever. The history and grandeur of the place were still overwhelming. Looking up at the structure, the ornate iron gates and lanterns, and the gorgeous stonework, he was suddenly flooded with emotion. He had fond memories there, though few and far between. Playing in the courtyard with his friends, occasionally meeting celebrities. The first time he kissed Annie was right across the street at the entrance to the park. As far as places to grow up in the city went, this was one of the best, in his opinion. But, the loneliness of being left with nannies in an apartment, no matter how beautiful, while his father worked sixty-plus hours a week had left him feeling neglected and resentful. Combined with his dad's general disregard of him in their daily lives, that indifference had created a strange, almost professional relationship between them. In high school, Wyatt had acted out, smoking pot, drinking, staying out all night, all in an effort to get his father's attention. Once, when he was seventeen, John had caught him in his room with a girl. "As long as you're safe," he had said, leaving the teenagers to their business. It wasn't until the hallucinations started that Wyatt's father seemed to take notice. It was his buddy's eighteenth birthday and Wyatt had stumbled in at around four in the morning, drunk off his ass after a long night of partying. He must have passed out on the couch, though he had no memory of getting past the doorway, let alone making it all the way to the sofa. A few minutes later, he was awoken by the sound of a woman crying. It was loud and filled the room, like an announcement over a loudspeaker. He felt hot, so he took his flannel off and dropped it on the floor as he attempted to find the source of the sobbing. It was dark in the apartment, no lights from the television, so he thought it must be a person. He had been proud that his father had finally brought a woman home but why was she crying? Was his dad a date rapist? Was he going to have to kick his own father's ass to protect some chick? He checked every room and found no one. Every room but one. He approached his father's bedroom door and hesitated for a moment while reaching for the doorknob. He knocked quietly before entering, hoping to find his father listening to some weird radio show and not abusing some poor woman.

What he found was his father asleep in his king-size bed, oblivious to the woman crouched in the corner of the room under the window crying her eyes out. She was wearing a long dress and her long red hair had half fallen out of its bun to cover her face.

"Dad," he had whispered. "Dad, wake up."

John rolled over and stretched. "What is it, Wyatt? What time is it?"

"Dad, what the hell?" he had said, gesturing toward the very obviously upset woman in his room.

John looked to the window. "What?" he had demanded.

"What did you *do*, Dad?"

"What are you talking about? Are you just getting home? Boy, it's almost tomorrow. You should be in bed."

"The girl, Dad!" Wyatt had shouted.

"What girl?" John asked, turning his bedside table lamp on. They both looked to the corner and they both saw nothing. She was gone. Wyatt didn't hear the crying anymore.

"She was right there," he had told his father.

"Damn it, Wyatt. Go sleep it off. Tomorrow, we're going to have a serious conversation about your behavior."

The next day, Wyatt drank coffee while his father lectured him about responsibility and thinking about his future. "You're almost a man now," He had bellowed. "It's time to get your life together." As he droned on, Wyatt again heard the woman crying.

"Do you hear that?" he had asked.

"Hear what?"

"The crying."

"The what?" John had asked. "Are you still drunk?"

"No, I'm serious," Wyatt had insisted. "You really don't hear it? It's *so* loud." Just then, he saw the woman standing in the corner of the kitchen wearing the same long dress, her hair still disheveled.

Wyatt jumped up from his seat at the island. "There!" he exclaimed, pointing her out. "She's right there! I told you I wasn't making it up."

John looked at the empty corner of the room and back at his son. As a lawyer, John had ample practice at snuffing out liars. He looked Wyatt in the eyes and knew that he believed what he was saying. John's annoyance turned to fear and the next few years were spent visiting doctors and psychiatrists, trying this and that combination of drugs and therapies. Nothing worked. The hallucinations continued. Besides the crying woman, Wyatt soon started seeing other people that weren't there, and they were all over. The apartment, the subway, on the street. While accepting his diploma at his high school graduation, he heard the woman's voice for the first time. *Where are you?* It had caught him so off guard that he'd nearly tripped. The nightmares came later, in college. His roommate complained about him screaming in his sleep so much that Wyatt was given a private room.

Senior year, he had come home for Christmas and while there, he had a particularly violent night terror. John had found him, eyes still closed, trying to rip up the floorboards in the living room with his bare hands while screaming, "Hang on! I'm coming!" The next day was Wyatt's first day at Clear View.

Wyatt did his best to push the memories from his mind as he made his way to his father's apartment. He was more than a little surprised that his key still worked. He knocked loudly as he walked in.

"Dad?" he called.

"Study," John called back.

Wyatt opened the door to his father's office to find him on the phone with what sounded like a client. John motioned for him to sit in the chair across the desk and held a finger up as if to say 'one minute' before taking a sip of coffee. *Guarantee there's bourbon in that.* Wyatt thought, remembering his father's habits. He looked just as Wyatt remembered him; sleeves rolled up, tie loosened, cleanly shaven. His father, just like the apartment, hadn't changed a bit.

"All right, Charlie, let me know if anything changes," John said to the person on the other end of the call. "You, too. Tell Elizabeth I said 'hello'. Goodbye." He hung up and took a good look at his son. He was still more muscular than John thought was necessary and his face had grown mournful like life had beaten him down. He supposed his mental illness and wife abandoning him were the cause of that and decided not to bring it up. No need to upset him.

"So, how was the trip?" John inquired.

"Fine," Wyatt answered. "How's your life?"

"Oh, can't complain. Work keeps me busy, as you know."

"No girlfriend? Wife?" he asked, noticing John still wore his old wedding ring.

"I have a wife," John snapped. "She just happens to be dead at the moment." They sat in awkward silence for a few seconds before John pulled out a file from a drawer and slid it across to his son. "Speaking of which," he said. "Your uncle, Spencer died."

"My what?" Wyatt asked, having no memory of an uncle at all.

"Your mother's half-brother. You only met him once or twice as a kid. You were probably too young to remember. He lived in Indiana, barely kept in touch. Anyway, he didn't have any children and his wife passed a few years ago, so he left his estate to you. There's his house, of course, in a town called Southport. Bank accounts and stocks that have been transferred to you. There are also a few rental properties and a donut shop he owned that belong to you now to do with as you see fit. You *will* have to call the bank to get debit cards."

Wyatt was flabbergasted. The contents of this file solved his money problems. He no longer had to panic-search for a job. "I don't know what to say."

"Not much *to* say," John said. "People get old, they get sick, then they die."

"Is that what happened to Mom?" Wyatt asked. "Did she get sick?"

"Wyatt," John cautioned.

"Come on, Dad. It's been decades. Why haven't you told me what happened? This place is like a goddamn shrine. There's at least one picture of her in every room but you've never talked to me about her. Not once. Why have you *never* told me *anything* about my mother?"

"Because," John said, his face a combination of enraged and heartbroken. "Talking about her kills me." He took another sip of coffee, set it aside, and pulled a glass followed by a bottle of scotch from his desk drawer. He poured himself a little and drank it, ignoring his son's disapproving glance.

"I'd just like to know what happened to her," Wyatt said to his father as calmly as he could. "I'd just like to know something about her. *Anything*. Please, Dad."

John was nearly shaking, he was so angry. "You want to talk about this?" he threatened. "You *really* want to bring up all this old bullshit?"

"Um," Wyatt answered, taken aback by his father's demeanor. "Yes."

"Fine," he said, taking another swig and slamming the glass down on the desk. "Abigail was perfect," he began, tempering his tone. "She was brilliant, and funny, and so goddamn beautiful, she didn't look real. She liked The Beatles, Queen, and Elton John. She liked to read and watch movies and complain that the book was better. She loved history, especially English history. Henry VIII, Elizabeth I, stuff like that. She made me sit through the whole royal wedding, Charles and Diana, you know. I was bored to tears, but I would have done anything she asked of me. That woman was my whole life."

He poured another glass and took a sip before continuing. "She was a real estate agent and a damn good one at a time when women weren't taken seriously in that field. She was tough, put up with a lot of shit that nowadays they'd call 'harassment'. While I was striking out on my own, establishing my firm, *she* was the one paying the bills. *She* was the one that got us into this building and paid the mortgage.

It wasn't easy, but she made it happen. This place was her dream. She worked hard, sometimes seven days a week, and she still had time to attend the events and dinners and bullshit elbow-rubbing functions I had to go to to get my name out there, form relationships with people that could potentially become clients. She was charming, graceful, poised. She was amazing on every level and it was because of her, because the fuddy-duddies and the DAR ladies all loved her so much, that my firm took off the way it did. In less than two years, I went from leasing an office to owning a building on the upper west side. She supported me and my dream and I always felt like I owed it to her to be successful, to put in the work to make it grow. Otherwise, what was the point of all her hard work and sacrifice?" He paused for a moment, bracing himself for what came next. "We had been so focused on our careers that we hadn't discussed when we'd have children. I knew she wanted them but it was always a 'someday' sort of thing. So, we were surprised when we found out she was pregnant but she was thrilled, and seeing her that happy made *me* happy. I was *so* fucking happy, I didn't recognize the signs."

"What signs?" Wyatt wondered.

John poured more scotch into his glass and took a drink. "Of her depression."

"Depression?" Wyatt asked. "You just said she was happy."

"She was. For a while. She put your nursery together, bought every toy in FAO Schwartz, I think. Spent hours in that room, just sitting in a rocking chair, rubbing her belly, singing to you. 'Hey Jude' on a loop. But, around the eighth month, she just stopped going in there. She stopped working altogether and started sleeping something like sixteen hours a day. I thought she was just tired from the pregnancy. She was edgy, easily irritated, but I thought that was normal hormonal crap. She complained that everything hurt. Again, it sounded normal to me. She was huge. Her back, her legs, her feet. It was all *supposed* to hurt. She stopped caring about how she looked, even when we went out. I wasn't about to comment on her appearance. I never bought into that whole 'pregnancy is beautiful' thing. It seems hard and miserable to me, so expecting her to be pretty during that time would have been ridiculous. Then, she stopped wanting to go anywhere. Ever. I wanted her to be comfortable in her last few weeks of pregnancy, so we stayed in. No big deal. But, then, she stopped reading. She stopped listening to music. That was *odd*, so I asked her about it and she said she 'just wasn't interested'. I called her doctor and he said it was 'baby blues' and it was fairly common and it would go away after you were born. It was maybe a week before her due date when she stopped eating. Said she wasn't hungry. At that point, I was worried. I did everything I could to get her to eat. I got her favorite take-out, bought all her favorite foods. Nothing worked. I got so frustrated, I tried to force a bite of pasta into her mouth. She threw the fork across the room and slapped me in the face. I was beside myself. I didn't know what to do." He paused. "You sure you want to hear this?" he asked his son. Wyatt nodded. John took another glass from the drawer, filled it with bourbon, and slid it across the desk. "All right," he began again. "So, one night, I get home from work, and the maid's freaking out, screaming something in Spanish. I don't know what she's saying, but she's banging on the bathroom door in hysterics. She runs up to me and the only words I can understand her saying are 'Mrs. Sinclair' and 'scissor'. So, I call to Abby to open the door but there's no response. So, I start kicking the door, trying to break it down. Finally, I throw all my weight against it and it opens." Tears started to pool in John's sorrowful brown eyes. Wyatt was getting nervous. He'd never seen his father show any real emotion *in his life.* John choked back the tears and did his best to still his voice. "She was on the floor, pale, not moving. There was blood and amniotic fluid everywhere. For a second, I thought she had gone into labor and passed out. But, then I saw the sewing scissors in her hand." He paused, clenching his jaw and taking a breath before continuing. "She had stabbed herself in the stomach, the doctor said eight times. She lost so much blood, by the time we got to the hospital, she was gone. They said it was a miracle you survived."

Wyatt stared at his father, stunned and speechless, and it was like he was seeing him for the first time. When he regained his motility, he picked up the glass in front of him and drank greedily until there was nothing left. He wiped away the tears that had fallen from his own eyes as he watched his father do the same.

"You remind me so much of her," John stated. "Smart, willful. Stubborn. You went off to New Jersey to be a fireman and I hated it. I mean, I *hated* it. But, I respected it. You did whatever the hell you wanted, just like your mother would have. Ballsy. It's strange. I look at her pictures every day and I'm fine. But it's always been hard for me to look at you."

"What?" Wyatt asked. "Why?"

"You never noticed?" John asked. "You look just like her. Your face is *her* face."

Wyatt looked at the picture of his mother that sat on his father's desk. He could definitely see the resemblance.

"There's a little bit of you in here, too, I think," Wyatt told him, pointing towards his eyes.

"You might be right," John agreed, taking another sip of scotch. The two men sat in silence for a while, both of them coming to terms with the conversation they'd just had. Wyatt understood now where his father had been coming from all these years. It didn't make him feel any better about their relationship but it did give him a certain kind of contentment. Knowing that there was nothing he could have done to change the way his father had treated him growing up, that John had his own issues that caused him to be distant and maybe blame Wyatt a little for his wife's death, was somehow comforting. His father was just a flawed, miserable, slightly alcoholic human being.

"Thank you for sharing that with me, Dad," Wyatt said. "I know that must have been really hard for you. I appreciate it."

"Yes, well," John said as if waking from a dream. He cleared his throat and composed himself. "*I* would appreciate it if we never spoke of this again."

"I concur," Wyatt teased.

"And there's the snark," John pointed out.

Wyatt laughed a little.

"I really am sorry about Annie."

"Thank you."

"All right, well, I have some work to do, so if you could lock up when you leave, that'd be great."

"Of course," Wyatt said, standing and making his way to the study door. "It was good seeing you, Dad. I'm glad you're well."

"Bye, Wyatt," John said, not looking up from the file he had just opened.

Wyatt took a quick glance around the room with its many bookshelves, filing cabinets, and paperweights. It all seemed smaller than it had when he first walked in. Less intimidating. He folded the file his father had given him and slid it in his jacket before pulling the door behind him.

"Bye, Dad."

"So, you're him, hmm?" Wyatt heard a voice from behind call to him as he exited the gates of his father's building.

"Excuse me?" he replied, turning to look at the slender Asian man addressing him. He wore a beautifully tailored suit, an oversized pair of sunglasses, and freshly polished shoes.

The man lowered his glasses to get a better look at Wyatt. "Yeah, it's you," he decided. "Come on." He began to walk, expecting to be followed. Wyatt stood in defiance.

The man turned back. "Did you not hear me?" he sassed. "Let's go before the princess loses her damn mind and starts screaming in ours."

"The girl," Wyatt said. "She sent you?"

"You know she did. For future reference, call her Gabriel. Anything else gets her panties in a twist. And, no, she's not a stalker. She told me that's what you're trying to tell yourself. I mean, homegirl can be overbearing as fuck, but a stalker she ain't. You coming?"

Wyatt followed the man across the street to the park.

"I'm Tae."

"Wyatt."

"Oh, that's cute," Tae complimented. "You're a tall motherfucker, aren't you? What are you, six-one?"

"Six-two," Wyatt corrected.

"Well, pardon me," Tae joked. "And those eyes. You must *slay*."

"You mind telling me where we're going?"

"It's just up here a little ways," Tae told him. "She thought you'd take the news better in a pretty environment. Before we get there, some things you should know. Bitch has a superiority complex because she knows every goddamn thing. She thinks she knows better than everybody and what's annoying about that is that she's right. You can't lie to her because she *knows*. Everything you've ever seen, heard, said, thought, or felt, she knows. Baby's telepathic, telekinetic, and pyrokinetic. She can heal the sick, raise the dead, and set up a duplex in your mind if she wants to. It's obnoxious."

I brought a picnic! Wyatt heard the woman say in his head.

"This bitch," Tae said. "Always gotta be extra. A *picnic*. I'ma have to tell her to reign it in."

Wyatt was dumbfounded. "You heard that?"

"Course I did. You're not the only one she pesters with that shit," Tae explained. "She's been chirping in my ear since Britney was still with Justin."

As they walked, they could see Gabriel sitting on some rocks in the distance. She looked up to meet their gaze and waved wildly as a huge smile stretched across her face.

"Now, listen," Tae warned. "She's about to tell you some shit you're gonna have a hard time believing. Trust me, when I first met her, I thought she was bat shit crazy. But, as fucked up as it is, it's all true."

Wyatt was more confused than ever as the two approached.

"Hey, girl," Tae said, taking a seat next to Gabriel and examining the contents of the picnic basket. "You really need to calm this shit."

"Raphael," she acknowledged.

"You brought a salad bowl of grapes and a jug of water," Tae griped. "What the actual fuck?"

Gabriel laughed and turned her attention to Wyatt. "Sit down, B," she said cheerfully.

"His name's 'Wyatt'," Tae told her as he munched on the grapes.

"I know," she said.

"You should probably call him that."

"Yeah, but I probably won't," she asserted before addressing Wyatt again. "Sorry your mom was animal crackers."

"Thanks," Wyatt said irritably as he sat across from the two in bewilderment. "Who are you people?" he asked.

"I'm Gabriel," she started. "This is Raphael. We're archangels, and, *surprise*, so are you."

"So you're deranged," Wyatt surmised.

"No, but I can understand why you'd think so," she told him. "You're not crazy, either, B T dubs. Just a freak show like the rest of us. Your real name's Barachiel."

Wyatt scoffed. "I'm an angel?"

"Archangel," she corrected. "Leader of four hundred and ninety-six thousand Guardians, Prince of Heaven, Angel of Blessings. You're kind of a big deal."

"Okay," he said, quickly standing up. "This is either some kind of scam, or you two are straight-up bats in the belfry. Either way, I'm out."

Gabriel tilted her head, staring at him blankly. Without altering her gaze, she raised her hand and flicked her wrist in the direction of some bushes that inexplicably exploded in flames, forcing a jogger to jump back and fall on her backside. Wyatt's eyes grew wide and his stomach dropped. He couldn't believe it.

"Come on," Gabriel laughed. "Burning bush?! That's *hilarious*."

"Was that necessary?" Tae snapped, grabbing the jug of water and rushing to put the fire out. "Pain in my ass."

Gabriel stood, giving Wyatt a knowing smile. "There's someone else you need to meet. She'll be able to clear things up for you a little bit."

Wyatt nodded, so overwhelmed by what just happened that he couldn't speak.

"You got this, Raph?" Gabriel called back as Tae struggled to put out the weakening flames.

"You best get the fuck out my face!" he called back.

She chuckled to herself as she led Wyatt out of the park. "Humorless, both of you."

Chapter 3

Walking along West 72nd Street, Wyatt took note of a sushi restaurant he'd never seen before.

"It wasn't here when you left," Gabriel told him, stopping several feet from the entrance. She smiled broadly. "There she is."

Next to the door was a pretty African American woman wearing jeans and a very large coat with several pockets. She looked somewhat perturbed as a man in a suit talking on a cell phone walked up, opened the door, and entered the restaurant. Behind him, an old man with a cane reached for the handle just as the door closed.

"Watch this," Gabriel said giddily.

The woman opened the door for the old man and followed him inside. After a few seconds, she reemerged, dragging the first man by his jacket. She snatched the phone from his hand and threw it in the street before opening the door of the restaurant once more, allowing a young couple to walk inside before letting go of the handle.

"How hard is that?!" she shouted to the suited man, who looked stunned and more than a little pissed off. He tried to retrieve his phone from traffic to no avail as he screamed obscenities in the woman's direction.

Gabriel was laughing so hard, she could barely breathe. "She's my favorite."

"Wyatt!" the woman exclaimed as she headed toward them. "It's so nice to meet you. You ready?"

"For what?" he asked.

"You didn't tell him?" the woman asked Gabriel. "I thought he'd be all caught up by the time you came to see me."

"You didn't tell me his dad was gonna take over an hour," Gabriel rebuffed.

"Bitch, I told you he was 'bout to catch him up on some family drama. That shit takes time," the woman said, turning her attention to Wyatt. She reached out for him to shake her hand, which he did. "I'm Valerie. Long story short, I'm gonna unclutter your brain a little. Help you distinguish what's normal and what's supernatural. What's a human voice and what's a ghost, stuff like that. I'm also gonna try to clean up those flashbacks you've been having so you can get some proper sleep."

"This is Uriel," Gabriel explained. "She's one of us. Divine visions, moral superiority, all-around badass. Today, though, she's gonna clean up what's going on in your head."

"I'm gonna try to," Valerie interjected. "But all those drugs you're on might make it difficult."

"You really need to stop taking that shit," Gabriel told him.

"For real," Valerie agreed. "Can we get going, 'cause I got a date in a couple of hours and I need to get home so I can get cute."

Gabriel chuckled as she attempted to hail a cab.

"So many things," Wyatt stated. "First, ghosts?!"

"Oh, yeah," Gabriel said. "Dead people are notoriously chatty."

"Yeah," Valerie chimed in. "You just have to ignore them. If they don't know you can hear them, they'll usually just go away on their own."

"Uh, huh," Wyatt said skeptically. "And, my nightmares?"

"Memories," Valerie corrected.

"Yeah, dude. That shit really happened," Gabriel informed him. "And before you ask, yes, we *really* want you to stop taking your meds because no, they're *not* helping you. They're just fogging up your brain, making it harder for you to see what's happening around you and making it impossible for me to find you. I've been looking for you since the turn of the century. Do you know how much easier things would have been if you had just answered me?"

Just then, a cab pulled up, but Gabriel shooed the driver away.

"No, sir, not you," she insisted. "You are already late for Izzy's recital and if you miss one more, Esperanza is going to stab you in your sleep. Go."

The cabby gasped, making the sign of the cross. "Bruja!" he shouted. "Eres del diablo!" He sped off, nearly taking out a pedestrian as he drove.

Valerie snickered. "Devil witch."

"He may be freaked out but I was serious," Gabriel told them. "His wife will literally murder him if he misses his kid's tap thing. That bitch is crazy."

"You know him?" Wyatt asked.

"No."

"That's gonna be your new nickname," Valerie laughed. "I'm gonna call you that from now on. Hey, Devil Witch!"

Gabriel rolled her eyes.

"What you been up to, Devil Witch?" Valerie continued. "DW Murphy, what's shakin'?"

"Okay, we're just walking," Gabriel conceded.

"Hey, Devil Witch, you got the time?" Valerie poked as she and Wyatt followed Gabriel.

A few blocks later, just past Broadway, they reached Gabriel's apartment. It was stunning. Entering through the double doors, the far wall directly in front of them was made entirely of windows. To their left was a kitchen with a large island and stools, marble countertops, and stainless steel appliances. To their right was a hallway with several doors next to a wall that housed a television that was at least seventy-five inches. Next to the kitchen was a set of french doors leading to a balcony where a table and two chairs sat. The cabinets, sectional sofa, and ottoman were all stark white which made the pink of the rosewood floors pop even more. Gabriel locked the door behind them and gestured to the couch. She got herself a bottle of water and leaned against the massive fridge.

"Go ahead, Uri," she commanded. "Fix him up so we can get the show on the road. We're already running late."

Valerie sighed. "It takes as long as it takes," she declared, annoyed with her sister's impatience. She sat on the sofa, patting the seat next to her. Wyatt joined her, not knowing what to expect, but feeling like nothing these women could do to him would be any worse than what he'd been living with lately.

"Just relax," Valerie instructed. "I'm gonna do all the work."

She put her fingers gently on his temples as Wyatt closed his eyes and took a deep breath. She took a few deep breaths of her own, not knowing what she'd see in there. Gabriel, as always, had been vague on the details.

She sorted through the haze of his still medicated mind for a few minutes before finding what she was looking for. She made quick work of mending his limbic system, allowing him to distinguish between normal and metaphysical beings as well as dreams and memories. One memory, though, she could see, was giving him particularly fitful nights. She decided to show him the memory in its entirety which would give him an understanding of it so he could move on.

Wyatt shuddered, suddenly feeling as if he'd been transported to another time and place. He was aware of everything going on in what he used to call his nightmare. Not only did he see and hear his surroundings, he could smell the air, feel the ground beneath his feet. And, he knew what was happening.

It was Verona, the year of The Consulship of Constantinus and Licinianus, and Constantine's forces had the city surrounded. There were men fighting everywhere Wyatt looked. Three different armies were battling it out in the city and the civilian population was getting slaughtered in the crossfire. As he watched in horror, an older woman quickly approached him, begging him to help her grandson. For the first time since he'd started having this dream, he could understand what she was saying. He followed the woman to an alley that was relatively quiet and they came upon a boy of about fourteen. He was lying there on the ground, the color drained from his face and bleeding heavily from the abdomen. His eyes had glossed over and were darting back and forth. He was almost gone.

The woman begged for his help, pulling on his clothes in desperation and despair. "If you can not save him, could you at least fetch some wine to alleviate the poor child's pain?" she pleaded.

Wyatt crouched down next to the boy and put his hand, which was much smaller and darker than his current one, carefully over the boy's wound. He looked up at the woman who stared, confused, and put his finger to his lips. She nodded and went silent, tears filling her forlorn eyes.

All at once, his hand and the wound underneath it began to glow. The boy's entire body began to glow as if it had been lit from the inside.

The woman fell to her knees in disbelief. She didn't know if this man was a good spirit or an evil one but if he saved her grandson, she didn't much care.

The wound slowly shrunk then disappeared completely and the boy gasped as if taking breath for the first time. He sat up, dazed, and stared up at Wyatt with stunned gratitude. Wyatt stood while the old woman hugged her grandson, kissing his cheeks repeatedly after inspecting the spot where his wound had been and seeing it was gone. She then began kissing Wyatt's feet and thanking him profusely. He lifted the woman to her feet and again put his finger to his lips. She understood. She would tell no one what had happened. Wyatt helped the two to safety before going back out into the war zone. There were more innocent people to be helped. Except, he wasn't Wyatt then and he knew it. Here, he was just Barachiel.

Wyatt's eyes flew open and he stared wildly at Valerie who had removed her hands from his head.

"Holy shit!" he exclaimed.

"Pretty much," Gabriel said.

"How did you do that?" he said, catching his breath.

"It's kind of my thing," Valerie bragged. "Now that you've seen it as a proper memory, it shouldn't keep you up at night. I also cleared up the confusion between your human side and the other. Now, when you see or hear a ghost, you'll know what it is." She stood to leave and headed toward the door while Wyatt just sat, still reeling.

"Shame you can't stay for dinner. I ordered pizza," Gabriel said, shifting her gaze to Wyatt. "You're welcome."

Wyatt couldn't help but laugh a bit. He had been dying for a slice since he got to the city and he was starving.

"Shame nothin'," Valerie told her. "I've been waiting on this man for *weeks*. He finally asked me out and I'm not missing this date for *shit*. Besides, this one's got questions. Now he knows this is legit and he's all kinds of freaked out."

Gabriel laughed. "Remember when I first found *you* and you pulled a knife on me? That was hysterical."

"I do," Valerie teased. "And, just so you know, I still carry that knife with me, so watch yourself."

"You know you can't hurt me," Gabriel scoffed.

"I know. But, I can sure as hell show my disapproval," Valerie taunted as she opened the door to go. "Hey, new guy," she said as she walked out. "Ask Big Sis about her boyfriend."

"That was super cunty," Gabriel quipped.

"See you later, ho," Valerie joshed as the door closed behind her.

Gabriel threw Wyatt a beer and sat next to him on the sofa, putting her feet up on the ottoman.

"I'm gonna let you ask your questions since it'll upset your sensibilities if I just start talking," she said, taking a sip of water.

"I appreciate that," Wyatt sneered.

"Go ahead."

"First," Wyatt wondered. "Who am I?"

"Barachiel, leader of the Guardian Angels, all of which are currently in heaven, obviously, but most of the time, you tell them where, when, and how to save certain people from certain things. Can be anything from not letting an old lady slip in her tub to stopping a bomb from going off in a building. You also create and control lightning, which is why you're here now."

"So, saving people is,"

"What you were made to do," Gabriel finished. "Your whole life makes sense now, doesn't it?"

He nodded and took a sip of his beer.

"But," Gabriel wanted to make clear. "Your existence as *Wyatt* is just as real and valid as it ever was. Your life has meaning and purpose aside from the bigger picture."

"And, Valerie?"

"Uriel, Angel of Hope and Divine Visions. Besides reorganizing your brain, she gets random visions. Some things that will happen, some that have already happened. She also leads souls into Heaven, and by that I mean she tries to get people to do the right thing, hence the phone in the street." Gabriel giggled. "Raphael's supposed to be the funny one but she cracks me up. Raphael is our best healer, which is why he became a doctor even though he had started a travel agency in college. He ended up selling the agency to pay for medical school. He's also the Angel of Happy Meetings, which is why I had him meet you at your dad's. He makes the best introductions."

"So," Wyatt said. "Angels are real, so that makes..."

"God," Gabriel confirmed. "Yeah, He's real. Not like most people think, I mean, He's complicated."

"Complicated."

"Yeah, it's like, he's *everything*," she explained. "The couch, the air, us. Every atom is part of God. So, He used to be this tiny little ball thing but he was bored and lonely, so he spewed himself all across the nothing and created Creation."

"Like the big bang?" Wyatt asked.

"Exactly the big bang," she told him. "So, think about everything in the universe like body parts. Cells in one unimaginably giant entity. And at the center of everything is God's consciousness, which I'll just refer to as 'God' from now on to make the conversation easier. Directly surrounding that is Heaven."

"His consciousness," Wyatt said. "So, he has like, a personality?"

"Totes."

"What's that like?"

"Oh, you know, self-righteous. Funny. He loves everyone and everything. He's basically a know-it-all father figure with a lot of dad jokes."

Wyatt laughed. "How do you remember this? Why don't I?"

"I don't actually remember it," she made clear. "It's more like I saw it in a movie or learned about it in school. I know this stuff like you know about Pearl Harbor. You don't *remember* it, but you can tell me what happened. And, while it seems like I do, I don't actually know *everything*. Just what God *wants* me to know. I'm His Messenger, so I know and relate pertinent information but there are a *few* things I don't know. For example, I have no idea if aliens exist. No clue. Could be none or there could be an alien city on the dark side of the moon. I'm oblivious. Fairies, unicorns, dragons, fucking Big Foot, I could not tell you."

"That's funny," Wyatt chuckled.

Abruptly, Gabriel jumped up and rushed toward the door. "Yay, pizza!" she sang just as there was a knock at the door. She opened it, smiling broadly. "Ethan, my precious," she said, pulling a twenty-dollar bill from her back pocket and handing it to the delivery guy.

"You don't have to pa--" the carrier stopped, seeing Wyatt who sat silently on the couch. "Who the hell's that?"

Gabriel tried not to laugh at Ethan's insecurity. "That's my brother, Wyatt." she snickered. "You don't see the resemblance?"

He looked Wyatt over suspiciously. "I guess you both have brown hair," he conceded. "So, I get off in a few hours. I was thinking, I could stop by and--"

"I know what you were thinking, sweetie, but it's not happening tonight," she rebuffed. "Family stuff."

"Okay, well call me when--"

"I'll call you sometime," she said, taking the pizza and closing the door. "Eventually, probably," she muttered as she placed the box on the island and opened it. She took a slice for herself and waved Wyatt over. They both sat and began eating.

"So, that's the boyfriend I'm supposed to ask about?" he baited.

"No, that's just Ethan," Gabriel said. "He helps me out sometimes. You know, sexually."

"Oh," Wyatt said, eyebrows raised.

"What?" she said, daring him to comment.

"I'm not saying anything."

"Mm-hmm."

"So, that's *not* the guy Valerie was talking about?" he asked, unable to stifle his curiosity.

"She wasn't talking about any one person in particular. She just has *opinions* about how I live my life, that's all."

"I see. So, is she worried about you or just nosy?"

"Thank you!" Gabriel exclaimed. "Bish all in my business and shit. I don't want a boyfriend. What's the point? Date some dude for so long he gets all attached and then one day I'm just like, 'Oh, by the way, I'm the fucking Messenger of God and I can't make it to dinner tonight because I have important saving the world shit to do. Sorry.' Or, I just hide who I am forever, and what kind of life is that? Keeping this secret would be like, effort, and I don't have room. Besides, when you know everything, pretty much *everyone* is too annoying to be around for more than a weekend."

"As long as you're safe, it's none of my business."

"Safe? What for?" she scoffed. "If I get sick, I heal myself. I can't get knocked up and I don't carry disease. Uriel just thinks I treat my partners badly by not ever committing to one. Says I might hurt their sensitive human feelings. But, I *know* what they're thinking and it has *never once* been 'Oh, I wish all this consequence-free sex came with more strings.'"

"All right, then," Wyatt said. "I'm sorry, though, about your fertility issue."

"Oh, I forgot to tell you," she realized, starting her second slice of pizza. "None of us can have kids. Like, ever. You boys are sterile and me and Uriel don't even get a monthly business. It doesn't suck."

"What do you mean, sterile?" he contested.

"Don't freak out, we're *angels*. We're *forbidden* from procreating, and when God forbids something, he doesn't trust people to do what he says. He just makes it impossible."

Wyatt could feel his life crashing down around him. Annie would never come back to him now.

"Hey," Gabriel said, rubbing his back. "In case you haven't noticed, I'm *loaded*. If you need money for adoption fees or a sperm donor or something, I'm here for you, bro."

"We just met."

"*You* just met," she corrected. "I've known you *forever*."

"Thank you."

"Don't thank me yet," she warned. "I can give you a fuckton of money but that's not gonna bring your girl back. She's not gonna believe you magically got better overnight. And, I think you know you can't tell her any of this angel stuff."

"No, she'd think I'm crazier than she already does," he agreed. "Out of curiosity, why won't God let us have kids?"

"History lesson," Gabriel started. "Back in the old days, when humans were new and interesting, some angels got obsessed. They possessed the bodies of men to see how being human felt, and you know what it's like to be in here. You're hungry and thirsty, everything hurts and half the time, you're desperate for ass. Nothing ever satisfies for very long and it's just constant satiation of these stupid animal instincts. You and I were born into these bodies so we're used to it, but these motherfuckers just stepped right into the shit and couldn't control themselves. Some of them started seducing and even raping chicks, which resulted in offspring we called 'Nephilim'. Half angel, half human, those monstrosities were *unmanageable*. First, all the women that gave birth to them died. Their power was too great for a fragile human body to take. The fetuses grew something like three times as fast as normal pregnancies and then, instead of a normal delivery, the baby would force its way out, tearing at, we'll just say, *all the things*. Once born, they grew fast. By the time three years had passed, they looked, felt, and spoke like they were in their twenties. They were geniuses, master manipulators, and they were strong as fuck. They had the powers of their fathers but with human souls and brains, so they were *unbalanced*. Some forced people to worship them like Gods.

Some went on murdering sprees. They were so hungry, they'd eat all the available food in a village and starve their neighbors to death. One asshole burned his whole town to the ground because the local winery couldn't make more wine because, after drinking it all, he ate all the grapes for miles. These abominations were fucking nuts. God eventually got sick of their shit, sent the angels that sired them to Hell and wiped the Nephilim from the Earth."

"How'd he do that?"

She took a sip of water before answering. "He made it rain."

"Oh."

"Yeah." She finished her pizza before speaking again. "After that, God took away our ability to breed, whether we be in a human host or otherwise."

"*Otherwise*. So, what are we *really*?"

"As angels, we're energy beings that don't really look like anything. We're invisible to humans unless we want to be seen, at which point, we can make ourselves look like pretty much whatever we want. Currently, the few of us that are here are occupying human bodies that would have died before birth. Had Wyatt Sinclair had a human soul, his mom's nutty-as-a-fruitcake moment would've killed him, and without you to be strong for, John would have spiraled into such hardcore alcoholism that he'd have lost his practice, his home, and he would have died penniless on the streets of cirrhosis in two thousand nine. Speaking of death, yes, we can die. We're basically human, our bodies just formed to be able to handle us. Because of our ability to self-heal, we probably have a longer than usual life expectancy, but we'll all ultimately die of old."

"I don't self-heal."

"Really?" she asked. "You ever get injured on the job? Smoke inhalation? When was the last time you were sick?"

Wyatt thought about it and couldn't remember. He recalled no instance of sickness in his life.

"Not even a cold," Gabriel stated. "Anyway, when we die, assuming we get cremated, we'll be pulled back to

Heaven like we're on bungee cords. Our bodies act as a tether keeping us on Earth. They get destroyed, we go home. Otherwise, we're stuck here, roaming this dump until the Gates open. Yeah, yeah, the apartment's great but it's a third-world gutter in comparison, trust me."

"Gates?"

"And, to the reason we're here on Earth now," Gabriel began. "A few weeks ago, God started his rest. Every seventh celestial day, a 'day' being two hundred and forty-three Earth years, God shuts down his consciousness. Heaven's Gates and the Gates of Hell slam shut and any angel or demon still on this planet snaps back like a supermodel after a pregnancy. The only thing in or out are human souls. It's His way of ensuring humanity's control over their own evolution. The system has worked like gangbusters for infinity except now, a particularly fucked up so and so has thrown a wrench in the works and Dad needs us to clean up the mess while he's taking a nap."

"How do we do that?"

"We'll talk about it. Listen, I'm gonna put the rest of this pizza up for later. I know you want to, so go ahead and call your wife. When you're done, we need to get to work."

"Work?"

"Training," she insisted. "You need to learn to control your lightning and get yourself ready."

"Ready for what?"

"Anything. Your room's the first door on the left. That's where you'll be staying for a while, so get cozy."

"Yes, ma'am," Wyatt said jokingly. He made his way to the bedroom where he found a closet full of clothes in his size and an en suite with a sticky note on the mirror that read 'You still owe me for Jersey'. He laughed out loud as he went back to the bedroom, took his jacket off, and threw it on the chair in the corner, pulling his phone from his pocket. He dialed Annie. No answer. For once, he was excited to leave her a message because, this time, he wouldn't be crying and begging her to come back. This time, he felt like he had legitimate good news to share, even if it was under odd circumstances.

"Hey, baby," he began. "I just wanted to let you know where I am, in case you went by the apartment and I wasn't there. I didn't want you to worry. I'm in the city visiting family. Turns out I have some. Saw my dad which was," he paused for a second. "Interesting. I, um," Tears began to gather in his eyes as he tried to choke back the quiver in his voice. "I was hoping maybe you'd give me a call back, just to check in. I miss you. Okay, bye."

He hung up the phone and sat for a while trying to collect himself. He wiped the tears from his face, his mind wandering from thoughts of Annie to what Gabriel had said about his father. He had always known that he was a huge disappointment to his dad but knowing that had it not been for him, John would've died years ago turned the tables on their relationship in his mind somewhat. He felt a new appreciation and responsibility for his father and for the first time ever, he felt glad to have been born.

Looking around at the room, queen-sized bed and nightstand on one wall, television opposite, he decided he might as well stick around and help out with whatever big bad was coming. While he didn't know what exactly Gabriel had in mind, if this lightning thing was for real, he was actually kind of excited to see what he was capable of.

Chapter 4

The man's eyes bulged as life slowly left his body. Allydia's grip remained strong around his throat until she was satisfied that he had expired. Once sure, she left his body on the satin sheets of the four-poster bed and put her gown back on. She left the bedroom, entering her throne room. It was one of many in this city but it happened to be her favorite. Beautiful settees and chaise lounges lined the walls which were covered in gorgeous paintings and tapestries. The center of the room was adorned with a rug from the old country that Allydia had always loved and at the back of the room, opposite the door, was her throne. Beautifully ornate carvings filled the wood and it had extra thick padding under the purple upholstery to make it as comfortable as possible. She sat, watching the others indulge in all manner of drug and debauchery, as an assistant poured her a glass of Shiraz.

"Was he not to your liking, Majesty?" the girl asked, peering into the room and seeing the dead man.

"He disappointed me," Allydia sighed. "Be a dear and ask your Governor to have someone dispose of that."

"Of course, Majesty. Right away."

The girl scurried from the room while Allydia took a sip of wine but before she could swallow, her Governor of New York rushed in.

"Out!" he shouted. "Now! Everyone out!"

The room emptied and as the last person out closed the door behind them, the Governor knelt on the rug before his Queen.

"What is it, Tobin?" she asked dismissively.

"There are reports, Your Grace," he said shakily. "Of the creatures you described. Six eyewitnesses."

Allydia sat up straight and moved to the edge of her seat. "Are these witnesses trustworthy?"

"I believe so, Your Grace." He was nearly trembling with fear as he gathered the courage to look her in the eyes. "What are your orders, Your Majesty?"

Allydia sat back and thought for a few seconds. "Stay clear of them," she told him. "Ignore them unless approached and if they *do* engage, fight dirty, because they will."

"Yes, Your Grace," he agreed, standing to leave. "I'll put word out."

"Thank you, Tobin. You may go."

Once alone, Allydia's concern turned to excitement. She brushed her long dark hair off her shoulders and drank her cup dry. It had finally begun, what she had been waiting for all these years. She poured herself another cup, took a sip, and smiled mischievously. Revenge would finally be hers.

Chapter 5

"Okay, so the first thing you have to understand is that 'lightning' doesn't just come from the sky," Gabriel explained. "You can use the electricity from anything to create lightning bolts with varying degrees of electric shock. For instance," She took a D battery from her pocket and held it up. "You can take the charge from a battery and use it to make a small shock. It's enough to get someone's attention but not really enough to hurt them. You can pull the electricity from a wall socket, taking as little as a lightbulb's worth or as much as the entire power grid. You can take the energy from clouds, car batteries, cell phones, or even just the static in the air. There are two ways to do it. The first is focusing your intent and *feeling* what you're doing rather than thinking about it. That takes time and patience to get down, neither of which I have currently, so we're going option two, emotional upheaval. All the pain, depression, anxiety, and whatever bullshit just pisses you off is what you're gonna think about and focus on. Not what's going on in the room, not what you think you should be concerned with. Every strong negative emotion you've ever had, that's what needs to be in your brain. When you feel that shit bubbling up like you want to punch somebody, that's when you let it go. We'll start with this battery. Look at it, close your eyes, and think about something that upsets you."

"I'll give it a shot," he said, closing his eyes. He thought about the conversation he'd had with his father. He thought about his mother and what she had done to them and to herself. *How could she do that? How could she try to kill her own ba--*

"Shit!" Gabriel yelped.

"What?!" Wyatt shouted, his eyes flying open.

Gabriel smiled widely, opening her hand to show him the battery. It was completely destroyed, looking as if it had exploded in her palm, which was scorched and bleeding.

"Oh, God! I'm so sorry," Wyatt said.

"It's totally fine," she said, dropping the battery on the floor where the two sat facing each other. He watched in disbelief as her skin slowly healed itself. "Now, try the outlet."

He looked at the outlet on the wall and thought about the call he'd just made to his wife. He thought about how he didn't know where she was or if she was all right because she refused to call him back. He let himself feel how much he missed her as tears began to build in his eyes. Just as he remembered he was supposed to close his eyes in order to better concentrate, a bright flash erupted from the wall, setting the white faux fur rug ablaze.

"Holy crap balls!" Gabriel exclaimed. She jumped up and grabbed the small fire extinguisher she kept in a kitchen cabinet and put out the fire. "That was awesome!"

Wyatt was dumbstruck.

"Maybe you should practice on the roof from now on," Gabriel suggested.

"Probably wise," he agreed.

"Next, we'll work on aim," she told him. "Shouldn't be too difficult. You're getting the hang of your ability *with lightning speed*." She flashed an open smile as if to say 'Get it?' which made Wyatt chuckle.

Her phone vibrated on the counter and she picked it up, smirking when she saw the number.

"Hey," she said to the person on the other end of the call. "About half an hour. Just me and Barachiel." She turned to look at Wyatt who had moved to the bar and was drinking a beer. She grinned proudly and told the caller, "I think he'll be just fine. K, bye. Looks like training's done for the night." Gabriel said, placing her phone back on the counter. "We gotta go. Come on." She quickly walked down the hall to Wyatt's room. By the time he caught up to her, she was already rifling through the closet.

"What are you doing?" he inquired.

"Getting your outfit ready," she said, throwing a pair of black leather pants on the bed.

"I'm not wearing that," he said.

"Yeah, but you are," she insisted. "Where we're going, this tee shirt and jeans thing you've got going is not gonna fly. You will stick out like a pussy hat at an RNC convention." She tossed a dark burgundy shirt and a black vest down next to the pants, picked up a pair of boots, and handed them to him. "Wheels up in ten."

The two now stood in the alley next to a nightclub, Wyatt watching with condescension as people in clothing as preposterous as what he was wearing filed into the large brick building with blacked-out windows. He had begrudgingly worn what Gabriel had chosen for him and while he was wildly uncomfortable, he now understood her reasoning. She, herself, had gone full goth with black lipstick and eyeliner, navy velvet mini dress with extra long flowing sleeves, fishnets, and knee-high boots.

"I look ridiculous," Wyatt complained.

"Yeah, kind of," she agreed. "I look like nineteen ninety-six but what are you gonna do? This is their jam."

Wyatt noticed what looked like cat eyes at the other end of the dark alley. As they drew closer, he saw that they were too high to be a small animal. Out of instinct, he raised his arm in front of his new sister to protect her.

"Oh, that's precious," Gabriel chortled. "Completely unnecessary but still, super cute. Listen, when the delegation gets here, keep quiet. I'll do all the talking. Now, I have every confidence that we can handle ourselves but we need to lay low, so to keep these things at a distance, I need you to look tough. Like, full-on resting dick face."

He shot her an annoyed glance.

"Yeah, just like that," she approved.

He rolled his eyes a little. "What do you mean, 'delegation'?" he asked.

"She means us," a man said. Stepping out from the shadows of the alley were three men and a teenage girl. "Hattie, sweetie," he told the girl. "Stamp our friends."

"Yes, sir," she said, hurrying toward Wyatt and Gabriel and placing a red circle stamp on the backs of each of their left hands.

"I'm Tobin Abney, I'll be escorting you to Her Majesty this evening," the man informed them.

"Gabriel. This is Wyatt," Gabriel responded.

"Charmed," the man said kindly. "Follow me and do your best to stay close."

As they filed in, Tobin and the girl in the lead, Wyatt and Gabriel in the middle, and the two other men in the rear, Wyatt couldn't help but notice the unnerving amount of attention they were getting. People stopped what they were doing to stare as they walked past. Even the music, which Wyatt recognized but couldn't quite put his finger on, seemed to quiet slightly as they made their way to the back of the club and up a spiral staircase.

"Don't mind them," Tobin told them. "They're just curious."

Be careful, Gabriel warned as they approached the VIP section. *She'll have you feeding her peeled grapes by night's end if you don't watch yourself.*

The young girl pulled back a velvet rope and stood aside, allowing the others to walk through. Once on the other side, Tobin put his hand up, signaling for the others to stop before taking a knee.

"Your Majesty, I present Gabriel and Wyatt, as requested," he stated.

"Thank you, Tobin," a sultry voice said from the darkness. As Wyatt peered into the room, he saw the same kind of animal-like eyes as before looking back at him. As the woman came into the light, he could see that they belonged to her and that they now appeared normal. She was stunning in a black ball gown with dark hair, full lips, and vaguely Middle Eastern or Mediterranean features. Wyatt felt drawn to her somehow and as he couldn't help but stare, he wondered what her skin tasted like.

"Dude," Gabriel said pointedly.

"Sorry," Wyatt whispered as he gathered his senses.

"Leave us," the woman instructed the delegation. The others left and Wyatt and Gabriel sat in a booth next to the Queen.

"So," she said. "You call yourself 'Wyatt'."

"Yeah," he acknowledged.

"That's lovely," she breathed. "Allydia Cain," she said, holding her hand out for him to take, which he did, resisting the urge, just barely, to press his lips to it.

"All right, kids," Gabriel interjected. "Can you flirt later? We're here for a reason."

"Of course," Allydia said. "Later."

Wyatt let go of her hand and reminded himself that he was married.

"Pfft," Gabriel let slip.

"Hey," Wyatt griped.

"I'm sorry," she apologized. "But, I wouldn't call what you are *married*. Separated is more accurate. But, you're right. It's not my business."

"It's temporary," he insisted.

"Oh, sweetness," Allydia asserted. "Everything is temporary. *Life* is temporary. If a woman is feeble-minded enough to leave a man as beautiful as you, she lacks the sense God gave her and is undeserving of your patience."

"Anyway," Gabriel said. "I'm assuming you called because you have news."

"Yes," Allydia told her. "There are credible reports of demon activity in the city. Six eyewitnesses claim to have seen them, all on the Lower East Side."

"Demons?!" Wyatt blurted.

"Yeah, dude, chill," Gabriel directed. "Thanks, Dia. Call me if you hear anything else."

"I will," Allydia said as her guests began to leave. "And, Wyatt, just some food for thought, if your wife regains her faculties and comes crawling back, begging for another chance, perhaps you'll forgive her indiscretion. In the meantime, however, you would do well to remember that you're free to have some indiscretions of your own."

"Oh, gross," Gabriel winced. "Let's go." She led Wyatt through the crowd and toward the exit. Once outside, she smacked his arm in protest.

"What?" he laughed.

"Ew," she said. "Listen, I'm not your keeper. You do what you want but I'm telling you, that girl is bad news bears."

Wyatt scoffed. "I'm not interested," he claimed. "Despite what you think, Annie *will* come back to me. She just needs some time. Once she sees that I'm not crazy, everything will be back to normal."

"I hate to break the news," Gabriel told him. "But nothing is ever gonna be normal for you again. Just because you're not *crazy* doesn't mean things aren't severely fucked up."

Chapter 6

"So, demons?" Wyatt inquired, sitting at the island and taking a sip of his coffee. He had let it go the night before because he was exhausted after an unreasonably long day and just wanted to go to bed but it was a new day and he *had* to know what he had gotten himself into.

"Apparently," Gabriel replied. "The Gates of Hell aren't closed like they should be and that can only mean one thing."

"What's that?" he wondered.

"Girl!" Valerie called out as she let herself into the apartment. She closed the door behind her and quickly took a seat next to Wyatt at the island. Gabriel poured her sister a cup of coffee and patiently waited for her to tell her story, even though she knew everything she was going to say as soon as she saw her.

"I had a vision last night and I already texted Tae cause I knew you'd want to talk to him about it since it involved the hospital and he said he's on his way but first, let me tell you about my date," Valerie continued. "*This man*, first, as soon as he picked me up, announced we were going Dutch, and that's fine, like, I'm an independent woman, I got my own money. But, *damn*, why you gotta blast that shit in my face as soon as I open the door? Like he thinks I'm a gold digger or something, trying to extort him for some pasta. Then, we're at dinner and he sent his food back *twice* because the edges of the plates weren't clean enough. I was like, 'For real? You know what kind of awful stuff they're doing to your food right now?' and he told me they wouldn't *dare* because he's a health inspector. I don't care if you're the *mayor*, if you're that rude to your waiter, you're getting a spit sandwich. So, dinner's over and we're in a cab on the way back to my place, and I had *no* intention of letting him smash at that point. Like, if you treat your servers like shit, I just don't respect you, you know? So, we're in the cab and that's when the vision hits, so I probably look kooky as fuck, just staring off into the distance and shit for a good minute and a half. And, when I come out of it, this motherfucker is *kissing the side of my neck*, all uninvited, so I pushed his face away and I'm like, 'Uh, uh. You are *not* getting in tonight.' and this dude *took it out* and said *I* needed to take care of it."

"Oh, my God," Wyatt said. "That's awful."

"Wait for it," Gabriel smirked.

"So," Valerie told them. "We were less than a block away from my spot, so I yelled, 'Stop the cab!' and the driver pulled over, I opened the door, punched this dude in the face, and threw a travel size bottle of lotion I keep in my jacket at him and said 'Handle your own shit, baby dick'."

Wyatt and Gabriel couldn't help but laugh while Valerie nonchalantly sipped her coffee.

"I'm just salty because dude is *fine*," Valerie confessed.

"Muffins!" Gabriel suddenly exclaimed, jumping up from her seat and rushing to the door. She reached for the handle as they heard the first knock. She flung the door open, snatched the box of muffins out of Tae's hands, and placed it on the counter. She opened it, picked one up, and took a bite before turning back to him, grabbing his face, and quickly kissing his cheek several times.

"I thought they'd please you," Tae condescended.

"Yeah, yeah," Gabriel dismissed. "All I eat is carbs. How am I so skinny? Do I know what vegetables look like? Anyway, now that everyone's here, we need to talk about what we're doing, like, on Earth, because the plan goes into motion *today*."

"*Today?*" Wyatt asked.

"Relax," she told him. "You don't need to do anything just yet except practice. Today is just step one, getting the band back together."

"Girl, what are you on about?" Tae wondered.

"Uriel, please share with the class what your vision was about," she requested.

"All right, so," Valerie started. "It was a hospital room and there was a blond dude in the bed with like, tubes down his throat and shit and he was familiar to me but I didn't recognize him. Like, I *should* have known who he was and I felt like, nervous. Like I needed to get him out of that place. No offense, T."

"Mm-hmm," Tae sneered. "I mean, I *am* set to pull the plug on a John Doe in a couple of hours. He has blond hair."

"Yeah," Gabriel interjected. "I can't let you kill that guy."

"Bitch, I don't *kill* people," Tae rebuffed. "This motherfucker has been brain dead for a month. I am simply unplugging a machine."

"Okay," she agreed. "But, when you do, I need to be there to wake his ass up."

"What for?" he asked. "He one of your *companions*?"

"Oh, God! No! Ew!" Gabriel grimaced. "He's our brother."

"Another one?" Wyatt asked. "Jeez, how many angels does it take to screw in a--"

"Blond hair," Valerie blurted out. Her eyes became saucers and her mouth hung open as the realization hit her. "Are you serious?"

"Even when I'm joking," Gabriel declared.

"Which one?" Tae asked through a clenched jaw.

"Raphael."

"Which one?!" he shouted.

She looked at him knowingly.

"Bitch, are you out your goddamned mind?!" he snapped. "Are you trying to get us all *killed*?!"

"Calm down," Gabriel commanded. "He's on our side. Besides, between Barachiel's lightning and my all-around awesomeness, we'll be fine."

"Somebody gonna fill me in?" Wyatt asked. "Who are we talking about?"

"Motherfucking *Lucifer*," Tae griped. "This crazy bitch wants me to wake up fucking *Satan*. Mm mm. I am *not*. Not a chance in Hell."

"Lucifer?!" Wyatt gasped.

"He's not what you think," Gabriel said. "Exactly."

"No, not *exactly*," Valerie confirmed. "But, he *is* terrifying as shit."

"Sure, but he always does his job," Gabriel insisted.

"We are talking about the *Devil*, right?" Wyatt argued. "How are we considering this?"

"All right, kids, listen up," Gabriel began. "Back in the day, Lucifer was God's favorite. Not just His favorite angel, his favorite *everything*. He was the most beautiful, most powerful, and the most dedicated angel in Heaven. God loved and trusted him above all others. So, when the angels fell and God created Hell as a place to lock them up to protect humanity and the world He'd created, He knew there was no one else that could guard the Gates but his number one. Now, Hell's a big place, so every once in a great while, somebody will make a break for it and he has to come top-side to fetch them but for the most part, Lucy keeps those bitches in line. With him trapped in this John Doe, though, you know, the mice will play."

"The demons Allydia was talking about," Wyatt surmised.

"Yep."

"You make it sound like he's a good guy," Wyatt said, puzzled. "If he's just trying to keep demons from hurting people, what's the problem? These two are on the verge of panic attacks."

"Being the jailer means you have to spend your time in jail," she explained. "Hell is *separation from God*. Being in that place with those vermin, away from us, away from Grace, over time has had an *effect*. Which is why we need to find the monster we're after as soon as possible, he can take her back to where she belongs, close the Gates of Hell, sucking all the demons back in," she brushed her hands together. "Crisis averted."

Wyatt, Valerie, and Tae sat in mind-boggled silence for a few seconds.

"We good?" Gabriel asked, looking around at everyone stubbornly.

"We are definitely not *good*," Valerie answered. "Knowing the psychology of why someone's a barbaric, brutal psychopath doesn't make it *fine*."

"We need him," Gabriel said pointedly. "He's the only one of us capable of putting this monster back where she came from."

"She? You don't mean,"

"Lilith," Gabriel said plainly.

"Holy shit," Valerie all but whispered.

"Oh, fuck me," Tae said, sitting down. "I'm gonna need something stronger than coffee."

"You two have a vague idea of who this bitch is, but B's oblivious, so let me break it down," Gabriel related. "Lilith is Lucifer's twin sister. Take everything you've ever heard about Lucifer, most of which isn't actually true, by the way, and evil it up by about five thousand times. In our current states, we can't kill her but we can weaken her enough that Lucifer can drag her baby eating ass back to her cage."

Wyatt nearly choked on a bite of muffin.

"Yeah," Gabriel continued. "Bitch fucking *eats* babies, like, as snacks. And that's just the tip of her bat shit iceberg. She's *heavily* into dudes and once she picks one, things get real dark real fast. Lilith is twisted on a level that the human race hasn't seen since the Bronze Age. I can not stress this enough, guys. We *have* to take her down and we need our brother to do it."

"It's still morning and I'm already done with today," Tae muttered as he took a sip of coffee.

"The plan is pretty straightforward," Gabriel told them. "We get Lucifer functioning and on board, Barachiel, you'll keep practicing, getting stronger so you can play your part when we need you, Uriel will hopefully get some helpful visions along the way, and I'll do my best to keep Lucifer on a tight leash. Eventually, Lilith will contact Allydia. When she does, assuming we haven't found her ourselves beforehand, Dia will give us a location and that's when we'll go after her."

"And Allydia is?" Tae asked.

"Lilith's step-daughter. It's complicated," Gabriel said. "Point is, she doesn't know that Dia goddamn *hates* her. She's our way in."

"All right, girl," Valerie reconciled, standing up and drinking the last bit of her coffee. "Let's get to it, then."

"B, you stay here and practice," Gabriel commanded. "You never know when Lucifer's gonna get rowdy. Best to be prepared, just in case. You two with me."

The others left quickly while Wyatt sat, stunned, trying to digest all the objectively insane information he'd just heard. Feeling the likelihood of his impending demise, he decided to call Annie, maybe for the last time. The phone rang several times and then, a miracle. She answered.

"Hi, Wyatt," she said quietly. He was dumbstruck. For a second, he forgot how to speak. "Wyatt?"

"I'm here," he replied, clearing his throat. "I just wasn't expecting...how are you?"

"Fine," she told him, but she didn't sound like herself. Something was off.

"Are you? You sound strange."

"I'm okay, Wyatt. What do you want?"

"I wanted to tell you that I'm doing a lot better. No seeing things for a few days now. I had a procedure. Annie, *no voices.* I swear, I think I'm gonna be okay now."

"That's great for you," she said, not really believing him. "I hope that's true."

"It is," he assured her. "Listen, I'll be in the city for a little while, not exactly sure how long. Family stuff. But, when I get some time, I thought maybe--"

"Wyatt," she cut him off. "There's someone else."

His stomach dropped. "What?" he choked out. "What are you--"

"I'm sorry," she said, her voice beginning to quiver. "I'm so sorry, but--"

"No," he begged, tears streaming down his face. He began to pace around the apartment, his body starting to tremble. "Baby, I'm better, I promise. You don't have to do this. Please."

"It's done," she made clear, her voice shaking. "Please don't call again."

The line went dead as did any hopes Wyatt had for a reconciliation. He could forgive his wife for being afraid of him. It was completely understandable. He had been a train wreck the last couple of months before she left. He could forgive her for wanting to lock him up in an institution. He could forgive her for leaving, given the circumstances but he *could not* forgive her for sleeping with someone else. Even if she came back to him right then, he'd never be able to get past it. That was it. His marriage was really over.

He dropped the phone and fell to his knees. The pain growing in his chest was intense. He was gasping for air and he felt like he might throw up. The combination of rage and devastation was overwhelming as he gripped his chest and tried to control his breathing. Overcome with grief, he let out a booming scream and as he did, he lost all control. The room suddenly lit up with a dozen lightning bolts erupting from every socket. Appliances exploded in sparks, light bulbs blew out, and curtains burst into flames. He saw the fire through his tears and, for a second, wondered if he should let it burn. Let the smoke that was filling the room fill his lungs and put him out of his misery. His life was over now, anyway. After a few moments, he decided against it, knowing that he had a responsibility to literally help save the world, not to mention the fact that there were other people living in the building.

He tore the burning curtain from the wall and stomped out the flames. He coughed as he opened the doors to the balcony and threw the charred fabric onto the patio table.

"Girl trouble?" Allydia asked.

Wyatt was taken aback. "Where'd you come from?"

"Near the Red Sea, originally," she offered.

"How long have you been out here?"

"Just a minute. I heard a ruckus."

"What do you mean, 'a minute'? That doesn't--"

"Can I come in?" she requested. "It's getting kind of chilly."

He noticed her gathering the oversized hood of her long coat around her face. She did, in fact, look cold.

"Sure," he accommodated.

"Thank you, Wyatt," she purred, slinking closely past him into the apartment. She looked around at the mess and back at Wyatt, who had come inside and sat down on the sofa. She watched attentively as he wiped away some stray tears from his cheeks and smoothed his hair back from his face.

"Gabriel's not here," he told her.

"Oh, I know," she admitted. "What I need, she can't help me with."

"What do you want, Allydia?" he sighed.

"Say my name again," she said, sitting next to him.

"Are you hitting on me right now?" he asked.

She slid closer. "You can't be surprised," she presumed. "You're spectacular. You have mirrors, right?"

"I'm flattered," he said. "But, my wife just told me she has a new boyfriend, so I'm not exactly in--"

"Well, you know what they say," she cooed, swinging her leg over him and climbing swiftly onto his lap. "When one door closes."

"Allydia,"

"Mm," she breathed. "Yes, darling?"

As he tried to resist her advances, the pain he had been feeling so strongly was now slowly giving way to something else. All thoughts of Annie, Lucifer, and Lilith vanished. Even the room around him seemed to fade. All he could see was her.

She took her coat off and threw it to the floor. "Do you want me to go?" she asked quietly, leaning in, getting her lips as close to his as she could without touching. She gently stroked his face and looked into his eyes. He couldn't think. The world had disappeared. She was all there was.

"Wyatt, do you want me to go?" she asked more firmly. He didn't. That was the last thing he wanted. In that moment, all he wanted in the world was her.

He stared into her eyes and shook his head, allowing his hands to wander up her thighs as she straddled him. She smiled as she ran her mulberry-painted fingernails over the stubble on his cheek. She delicately brushed her lips to his and dragged her fingers through his hair. As he pulled her skirt up, he could feel she wore nothing underneath and began kissing her more deeply. With little effort, she quickly unzipped and removed his jeans along with his boxer briefs and set herself upon him again, this time placing him inside her. He tore open her blouse, sending buttons flying in all directions and exposing her full breasts, which he began kissing. His lips moved up her neck as he squeezed her backside. She writhed on top of him, her body quaking with pleasure. She grabbed the back of his head, gripping his lush dark hair and pressing his mouth harder against the side of her throat. They went on this way for a long time, both of them never having felt bliss like this before. He wrapped his arms around her, pressing her even closer and grunting with ecstasy as he came inside her. She gasped, her own climax exploding with sheer rapture. She could no longer hold back. Her eyes dilated completely and her fangs began to grow. Before she could stop herself, she clamped down on his neck, piercing his carotid, and allowed the sweet warmth of his blood to fill her mouth. She swallowed hungrily, unable to restrain herself.

The pain of the bite cleared Wyatt's head as if he were coming down from a high. "Stop," he said, trying and failing to push her off. "Allydia, stop!"

She didn't.

"Allydia!" he pleaded, his hands beginning to feel cold.

Again, she ignored him, grasping the other side of his neck.

The cold feeling was spreading to his arms and legs. He felt weak and a little numb.

"Allydia, get off!" he shouted, lightning spewing from his hands, throwing her across the room and into the wall. She fell to the ground and stood, smiling fiendishly as she looked up at him before wiping her bottom lip.

"I'm sorry," she claimed. "I couldn't help myself."

"What are you?!" he asked, pulling his pants up and putting his hand to his throat.

"I've been called a lot of things. 'Alukah', 'Estrie', 'Succubus'."

"You should go," he insisted.

"If that's what you want," she complied. She retrieved her coat, backed out of the apartment, and gave him a wink before closing the door behind her.

Wyatt finished getting his pants zipped and buttoned while looking around at the damage he'd caused. All of the appliances were destroyed. The television was hanging from the wall by its cords, which were fried. The can lights were all blown and there were scorch marks everywhere. He would do his best to clean up the mess but he knew Gabriel was going to be pissed.

He went to the bathroom to check out his neck. What looked like an animal bite slowly healed itself as he looked in the mirror in awe. He washed the blood from his skin and took off his blood-soaked shirt, looking, flabbergasted, at his reflection. "What is my life?"

Chapter 7

"So, how come he always takes up in a blond dude?" Valerie asked as she and Gabriel stood over the John Doe. The man looked fragile and weak, utterly helpless. But, Gabriel knew better. Once she undid whatever magic Lilith had done and Lucifer was awake and in control of the body he was in, he'd barely be manageable. She was banking on the fact that he hated Lilith more than he loved mischief, but she knew she'd have to keep a close eye because he wasn't exactly rational.

"He had a thing for Vikings back in the day," Gabriel explained.

"Did he like playing pirate or was he just down for killing lots of people?"

"Neither. He was up looking for an escapee and some Nordic villagers gave him beer and taught him how to play Nine Men's Morris."

"Booze and board games?" Valerie chuckled.

"I have cases of beer and a closet full of games and you know I didn't buy that shit for myself."

"I hope it keeps him occupied because I for damn sure don't want to find out what kind of trouble he'll get into if he's bored."

"No, you do not, ma'am," Gabriel agreed. "You should probably back up."

Valerie quickly shuffled away to stand next to Tae who was guarding the door to the room.

"You didn't give him an x-ray?" Gabriel accused.

"I did a CT scan of his brain, which is *procedure*," Tae rebuffed. "Are you a doctor now? You want to tell me how to do my job?"

Gabriel raised an eyebrow. "Course not," she told him. She held her hand up and suddenly, something burst out of John Doe's chest and flew into her waiting palm.

"Holy shit!" Valerie cried.

"What the fuck is that?" Tae stammered.

Gabriel looked at the blood-covered object in her hand.

"Amulet," she told them. "Old Aramaic binding spell. It's what's been keeping Lucifer trapped. Pull the plug."

"Oh, Lord, please do not let me regret this," Tae said.

"You know He can't hear you, right?" Gabriel bated.

"Bitch, can you *just*?" Tae yelled as he pulled the feeding tube from the man's throat. He flipped the switches on the machines, shutting everything down, and waited for the monitor to flatline. Once it did, he edged his way back to the door. "It's done."

"Get ready, kids," Gabriel said, tossing the amulet to the floor. "Shit's about to get real."

She stomped on the faience bobble, crushing it to dust, and waited. The three stood with bated breath for several seconds.

"Is that it?" Tae whispered. Valerie shrugged. All at once, the man leaped up in his bed, eyes open wide, gasping for air, the wound on his chest healing itself closed.

Gabriel rushed to his side. "It's all right," she said. "You're okay."

"Sister," he said, amazed. "How long has it been?"

"I have no idea," she laughed.

"Well, you look," he paused, looking her up and down. "Nearly human."

"Nearly," she agreed.

"Where is she?" Lucifer demanded. "Where is that jealous, miserable witch?"

"We don't know yet. Close, though, it looks like."

"What happened?" Valerie asked shakily.

"Uriel," he said. "It's good to see you. How did I become trapped in this wretched, albeit handsome, animalistic form? I was hunting a demon who'd escaped during, let's say, an *altercation.* I knew Father would be closing the Gates soon, so it was a nice excuse to pay one last visit to His Creation before being banned. I indulged in a drink and then, just as I almost had the creature in my grasp, there she was, hardly able to control her laughter as she did her vile magic, securing me in this body and cursing me to a never-ending slumber. Like a ridiculous fairy tale."

"You don't know how she got out," Gabriel stated, clearly disappointed.

"No," Lucifer admitted angrily.

"Lucifer," Tae said quietly.

"In the flesh, apparently. Nice to see you, too, brother."

"Why are you British?"

"I'm not *British*," Lucifer corrected, slightly annoyed. "I'm simply speaking the language of those around me, only properly. Now, be a lamb and get big brother some water. I'm quite parched."

Tae nodded and quickly left the room, relieved to get a break from the madness within. He got a cup from the nurses' station and poured some water into it.

"Hello, doctor," said the nurse behind the counter happily.

"Hi, Nurse Bowen. How are you today?"

"Oh, just fine," she responded. "Packing up my youngest for college. Time flies, doesn't it? Do you have children, Dr. Iha?"

"No."

"Good. Don't," the nurse warned him. "They're terrible. You'll spend all of your money on the best private schools only to find out they threw away their acceptance letter to Yale and decided to go to the University of Albany to follow their dumbass boyfriend who's majoring in Art History. What kind of job does a degree in Art History get you, doctor?"

"I don't know."

"No one does."

Just then, the phone rang. The two waved goodbye to each other as the nurse picked it up and Tae scurried off back to the room.

"Thank you, Raphael," Lucifer said as Tae handed him the water.

"No problem," Tae said with a hint of sarcasm. "Now, you all have to get out of here before someone notices you. I'll do the paperwork to make sure everything looks like it was done on the up and up because you know I'm not about to lose my job over this bullshit, but you've got to *go*."

Gabriel placed a duffel bag on the bed and closed the curtain around it so Lucifer could get dressed.

"You sure about this?" Valerie asked.

"Yeah," Gabriel confirmed.

"I'd be careful if I were you," Tae told her. "He *is* the motherfucking Devil."

"You know this drape isn't enchanted," Lucifer said from behind the curtain. "I can actually still hear you."

Gabriel giggled, the other two shooting her glances of derision.

"What?" she said through her laughter. "He's funny."

"What the actual fuck?" Gabriel griped as she walked through the door of her apartment, Valerie and Lucifer filing in behind her.

"I'm sorry," Wyatt told her.

"If this is what happens when he uses his powers, why aren't you having him practice somewhere else?" Valerie wondered. "Like an abandoned building or deserted island or some shit."

Gabriel looked at Wyatt, becoming aware of everything that had happened while she was gone.

"He just had a bad day," she decided. "It's fine."

"Barachiel," Lucifer said with a smile, walking toward him with his hand outstretched. "You're a fine mess. Human life not as worthy of saving when you're down in the muck, is it?"

"Probably not this one," Wyatt conceded, shaking his hand. "Lucifer, then?"

"Who else?" he quipped. "Well, you're not afraid of me at all. I'm impressed. Gabriel isn't, either, but she knows that she's my favorite sibling. Uriel, on the other hand, can barely keep her bladder in check. Seems she's caught a glimpse of some of my more rambunctious endeavors in a vision or two."

He glanced back at Valerie. "Don't worry, love. I'm no danger to you. Scout's honor."

"So, I'm gonna go," Valerie announced. "If I have a vision, I'll call."

"Okay, but don't waste time with a phone," Gabriel told her, pointing at her temple.

"I got you," Valerie called back. She was already out the door.

Gabriel reached for her phone as it rang in her pocket and answered. "Hey," she said. "How reliable is this guy? Okay, keep me updated." She put the phone back in her pocket before addressing her brothers. "That was Allydia. She said one of her guys has tracked a few of the demons to an abandoned theater on Canal Street. She's sending a few guys tonight to check it out."

"Allydia Cain?" Lucifer asked. "How is she? Did you send her my love?"

Gabriel rolled her eyes. "All right," she said, ignoring his questions. "I'm gonna go get lunch because I know you're both starving. Lucy, I need you to stay here with B until I get back. Lilith knows what you look like, so if we're gonna maintain our element of surprise, you have to keep a low profile, cool?"

"Of course," he told her. He then stood very close to her and leaned in, speaking almost in a whisper. "But let us be clear, I take orders from *no one*. I will happily do as you ask as long as I see the benefit but I will not be controlled. And, my name is *Lucifer*. I understand it's your way of maintaining a certain distance, not using the names people choose to call themselves. Fear of intimacy and such. But, if you call me 'Lucy' one more time, I may be obliged to rip your throat out with my bare hands."

Wyatt grabbed him by the arm to pull him away but Gabriel had the situation well handled. She made a squeezing motion in the air with her left hand that sent Lucifer to his knees. He clutched his chest, blood beginning to dribble from his mouth as he gurgled, trying and failing to breathe.

"I don't like threats," she said. "We're all here, serving our purpose, playing our parts in God's production. We're on the same side, yeah?"

Lucifer nodded.

"And we're gonna have a nice, pleasant relationship while we're here, right?"

Again, he nodded.

"Awesome," she said chipperly, kneeling to look him in the eyes. "I realize that I tend to take things over and I come off as a little overbearing but I've been working on this plan since the fucking Fall, and if your ego gets in the way, I will figure out a way to deal with Lilith without you, do you understand what I'm saying?"

He nodded once more, his face turning a strange shade of purple.

"Great," she said, standing and relaxing her hand.

Lucifer coughed and took deep, labored breaths as he struggled to stand himself.

"Since it's so important to you, I'll call you 'Lucifer' from now on, okay?" Gabriel promised.

"It would be much appreciated," he told her, clearing his throat.

"Now, I'm going to get lunch and call some people to handle this mess. You boys play nice."

As she left, Wyatt couldn't help but snicker under his breath.

"What's funny?" Lucifer asked angrily as he took a seat at the island.

"Nothing," Wyatt lied, unable to control his laughter.

"Shut up," Lucifer demanded.

Wyatt settled himself. "So," he said, changing the subject. "You know Allydia?"

"I know her," Lucifer smirked. "Occasionally."

Wyatt felt a twinge of jealousy at Lucifer's innuendo but he ignored it.

"Have you met the others?" Lucifer wondered. "They worship her like a deity. It's obscene. Enlighten me, what's Earth like these days? It's been fifty years or so since I was last hereabouts."

"Uh," Wyatt answered. "Loud, stressful, overpopulated. What's Hell like?"

"Same."

They both chuckled a little.

"Beer?" Wyatt offered.

"Please," Lucifer replied.

Wyatt opened the refrigerator door and it fell to the ground, spilling leftovers and condiments all over the kitchen floor, while the light inside sparked and burned out.

Wyatt sighed. "It kind of got away from me earlier."

Chapter 8

Tae sat alone in his office, still shaking from the events of the day. *Lucifer*. He couldn't believe it. He wrung his hands anxiously as he considered all the ways things could go bad. What was the *literal Devil* capable of? Mass murder? Genocide? Triggering the Apocalypse?

"She knows what she's doing," he told himself, trying to trust that Gabriel's plan would work and that she could keep Lucifer well managed. "She *always* knows what she's doing."

Just as he let out a deep breath and felt like he was starting to calm down, the desk phone rang, startling him to jump in his seat. His hand flew up to his chest so fast, he physically hurt himself. He felt ridiculous as he reached for the handset.

"Dr. Iha," he answered. He put the call on speaker, his hands again trembling too hard to keep the receiver steady.

"Yes, hello, Dr. Iha," the woman's voice on the other end replied. "This is Headmaster Olivia de Barde at Emerson Academy. You're listed as your niece, Michelle Iha's emergency contact when her mother is unreachable."

"What's the emergency?" he asked, standing up as dread began to set in. The possibilities flooded his brain. School shooting, fire, kidnapping. His niece was the only human family he had left since his brother died in combat a few years before. At Reo's funeral, he had promised Michelle that he would do everything he could to make sure she had the life his brother had wanted for her. He sent her mother money every month for whatever they might need and he spent every other weekend with her so she'd still have a positive male role model in her life. And, he enrolled her in and paid for this stupidly expensive private school to give her the best education possible. She had become like a daughter to him. If the people he trusted to teach and protect her had let something happen to her, there would be hell to pay.

"Dr. Iha, I hate to be the one to inform you," the woman said. "But, Michelle's mother was killed today. Her car was involved in a crash. One of the officers let it slip that it was the fault of the other driver who failed a field sobriety test. I'm very sorry."

"Oh, my God," Tae uttered, falling back in his seat. Relief washed over him followed by sadness and worry. "Does Michelle know?"

"Yes, the school's counselor is with her now. She's taking it pretty hard, understandably. She's asking to go home early."

"Of course," Tae told her. "I'll be right there." He quickly ended the call, took off his lab coat, and looked at the clock. He left his office, throwing his jacket on as he walked.

"Nurse," he said as he passed the nurse's station.

"Yes, Doctor?" Nurse Bowen answered.

"I have to leave. Family emergency," he explained. "Can you please find someone to cover my rounds?"

"I'll do my best. Is everything all right?"

"Not even a little bit," he said as he hurried out the doors.

Tae rushed into the school and beelined it to the Headmaster's office where he was greeted by a man in his late twenties wearing a nicely tailored suit. The nameplate on his desk read 'Headmaster's Secretary, Harrison Marlowe'.

"Can I help you, sir?" the man inquired.

"Yes, hello," Tae replied. "I'm Tae Iha. I'm looking for--"

"OMG, of course," the man said jumping up from his desk. "Right this way." He ushered Tae into the Headmaster's office, looking him up and down as they walked.

"Have a seat." He gestured to a small leather chair facing a large desk. "She'll be right with you. Can I get you something? Water? Tea?"

"No," Tae declined. "I'm fine, thank you."

"Yes, you are," the man flirted, pulling a card from his pocket. "If you need *anything,* you just let me know."

Tae took the card. "I will do that," he said, watching the man walk out.

"Well, that was inappropriate," Tae whispered to himself. "Boy was sexy, though." He patted his knees as he impatiently waited, growing more nervous with every passing moment, knowing that he would have to somehow comfort his niece who had now lost both parents. He couldn't imagine how devastated she must be.

After what seemed like forever, Headmaster de Barde finally entered the room with Michelle following closely behind. The eighteen-year-old was very obviously heartbroken, her face sullen with remnants of smeared mascara still clinging to her cheeks as she dragged an overfilled book bag behind her.

Ms. de Barde shook Tae's hand. "Hello, Dr. Iha. Again, I'm so sorry for your family's loss." Michelle stood silently in the corner by the door, tucking her hair behind her ear and staring at the floor.

"Thank you," he said quietly.

"We were all just so sad to hear," she went on. "With her father gone and being one of only a handful of colo--" she stopped herself and cleared her throat before continuing. "*African American* students, things were hard enough on poor Michelle as it was."

"I'm sorry, but *what*?!" Tae asked heatedly. "Were you about to say '*colored*'?!"

The Headmaster shuffled quickly behind her desk and sat down.

"I'm sorry," she apologized. "As you can imagine, it's been quite a day."

"Uh, uh," he said. "You can not just gloss over the use of a racial slur. You are a grown woman. You know 'colored' is not acceptable."

"Yes, of course, you're right. I apologize."

"And she is not 'African American'. She is simply *American*. She was born in this country, as were her parents. Moreover, you didn't even get her ethnicity right! Her mother is Barbadian and her father, my brother, was Japanese, as evidenced by this beautiful Asian man sitting before you. If you're going to insist on categorizing people based on their race, you could at least use the term 'biracial' if for no other reason than accuracy."

"All right, Dr. Iha," she said, clearly getting annoyed. "Now, will Michelle be staying with you, or is there another family member that will be stepping in? We need to know who her legal guardian is now, for paperwork, you understand."

"Yes, she'll be staying with me," he replied coldly.

"Excellent. Now, our standard absence allowance for grieving is two weeks. Michelle has all of her assignments so she won't fall behind while she's out. Please make sure they're all completed before she returns."

"Damn, bitch!" Tae exclaimed. "You're not only *racist*, you're also *ice cold*."

"Excuse me?!" she gasped.

He stood, slamming his hands on the desk and looking the sixty-something-year-old woman in the eyes.

"This little girl's mother just died," he seethed. "Her daddy passed not too awful long ago and now all she's got in this world is me. Now, I may be goddamned amazing, but I am certainly not an adequate replacement for a teenage girl's momma. She is heartbroken and you have the indecency to sit there and demand she do *homework*?! Fuck that."

He turned and walked toward his niece, putting his arm around her. "Come on, baby," he told her. "You take as much time as you need." He glanced back at the Headmaster who sat in stunned silence. "There won't be any problems. I'm sure Olivia here wouldn't want the other parents finding out that she's an insufferably racist bigoted piece of shit, would she?"

Ms. de Barde opened her mouth to speak, but no words would come.

"Mm-hmm," Tae stormed out of the office, all but carrying Michelle with him. Harrison gave an approving slow clap as they passed, having heard the entire conversation.

"I'ma hit you up later," Tae said, looking back at the secretary as he and Michelle exited the building.

They had only made it a few steps when Michelle dropped her backpack, covered her mouth, and burst into uncontrollable tears. Her knees went weak and she nearly collapsed, save for her uncle taking her in his arms.

"I know, baby, I know," he said softly, holding her close and petting her hair. "You let all that shit out."

Bitch, you better not need shit from me for a while, he thought to Gabriel. *I've got other priorities.*

Chapter 9

Wyatt lay in bed, staring at the ceiling, unable to close his eyes, much less sleep. His wife, the love of his life and best friend was sleeping with another man. Yes, she had left him and maybe he should have seen it coming, but he hadn't. He was so sure that he could mend things between them at some point and now that that hope had been so cruelly extinguished, he was completely broken. The thought of Annie with someone else made his blood boil. How could she do this? And so *soon*. Was she having an affair before she left? How long did it go on? Was it someone he knew? Then there were the other events of the day that he couldn't stop thinking about. Between Allydia and Lucifer, he was feeling overrun by monsters. *I live in a freak show.* He thought.

Don't be so dramatic, he heard Gabriel's voice in his head. A few seconds later, she entered his room, sat in the chair, and covered her legs with the blanket she had wrapped herself in.

"Dramatic?" he retorted, sitting up in bed and switching on the lamp that sat on the nightstand. "Satan is sleeping in the room next door and I'm pretty sure I had sex with a vampire today."

Gabriel laughed. "You totally did. I tried to warn you."

"You didn't tell me she was a fucking *vampire*, or that vampires even *existed*."

"All right, my bad," she said sarcastically. "Next time, I'll be more specific about what *kind* of monster a bitch is."

"I'd appreciate it," he quipped. "Hey," he said, his tone more serious.

"No," Gabriel answered before he could ask. "I didn't know about your wife's new dude. I've never met her so I don't have access to her database, as it were."

"But, if you *did* meet her,"

"Yeah, I could tell you anything you want to know. I can track her down if you want."

Wyatt thought for a moment, then decided it was a bad idea. "Better not," he conceded. "It would probably just piss me off worse."

"Yeah," she agreed. "'What if' is generally better than confirmation of worse-case scenario."

"It doesn't matter. Before or after she left, she's still with someone else and she's still gone and without her, I'm--"

"What?" Gabriel prodded. "You're what? I will tell you. On one hand, you're Barachiel, leader of the Guardian Angels, Protector of Humanity, saving lives basically since people were *invented*. Arguably the most important angel in Heaven. On the other hand, you're Wyatt Sinclair, a little fucked up, but relatively normal dude that just found out he's got superpowers and is on a mission from *God* to save the fucking world. So, your ex has a boyfriend now. Fuck her. Shit gets a little dicey and she bolts? Fang bitch was right. She doesn't deserve you. *What are you* without a selfish, panicky, whiny, thirty-five-year-old toddler? Better off. You're an archangel, you're a goddamn superhero and you're my brother." She scooted to the edge of her seat and wrapped the blanket tighter around herself, looking Wyatt in the eyes. "I know we're not exactly a *normal* family," she admitted. "But, we *do* care about you." She stood and shuffled towards the door. "I know how you feel, like, literally, but you're not alone. Except for right now, because it's almost four in the morning and I'm sleepy as balls. Try to get some rest, okay? Your obsessive thoughts are keeping me up."

Wyatt chuckled. "I'll try."

"Night."

"Night."

As she closed the door behind her, Wyatt turned off the light and lay back down. He was touched by his new sister's words and he let them give him comfort as he closed his eyes and, after several minutes, fell asleep.

The next morning, Gabriel, Wyatt, and Lucifer sat around the kitchen island and had coffee and donuts from the shop around the corner.

"Some guys are going to be here in a few hours to fix all this," she informed them. "So, best behavior."

"Really?" Lucifer griped. "I quite like the place as it is. Reminds me of home."

"I'll pay for the damage," Wyatt offered.

"Don't," Gabriel refused. "I have a stupid amount of money. It's not an issue."

"How exactly did you acquire your wealth, sister?" Lucifer wondered, taking a sip from his disposable cup. Wyatt had been curious about that, too, but didn't think it would be polite to pry.

Gabriel swallowed a piece of donut before answering. "I inherited it."

"So, the humans that birthed you met an early demise, did they?" he sneered.

"Don't be a dick," Wyatt warned.

Gabriel sighed, visibly irritated to be talking about this. "Yeah," she said simply, shooting Lucifer an annoyed glance and taking another bite of her breakfast.

"Not going to elaborate, then?" Lucifer pushed.

"No," she flatly stated.

"What about you, brother?" Lucifer asked, shifting his attention to Wyatt. "Any interesting stories to share? Life happenings or goings-on? Anything you'd *bloody* well like to talk about?"

Lucifer and Gabriel quietly giggled as Wyatt irritably put his cup down.

"You told him?" he questioned his sister.

"No," she said defensively. "He figured it out on his own. You had some sort of micro-expression yesterday when you two were talking. Remember, he's *crazy*, not stupid."

"I prefer the term 'eccentric', thank you," Lucifer asserted. "So, are you and the vampire queen planning a spring or summer wedding? I assume it won't be too terribly soon, since we're all currently preoccupied with the plot to destroy her step-mother, not to mention winter in New York can be brutal. The traffic alone. The tourists, everyone scrambling to see trees and such."

Gabriel couldn't help but laugh.

"That's not funny," Wyatt said, struggling to keep a straight face himself.

"It's pretty funny," Gabriel said.

"Just mind the fangs," Lucifer jibed. "Certain acts can very easily become quite unpleasant."

"Oh, gross!" Gabriel exclaimed, covering her ears. "No, no, no. New subject."

"Did Allydia get back to you about the theater?" Wyatt asked.

"Yeah," she answered. "Her guy said he saw some people milling around, cleaning it up, but no Lilith."

"Okay, but how would he know? Couldn't she look like anyone she wanted?"

Gabriel and Lucifer looked at each other knowingly.

"You want to take this one?" she requested.

"Why not?" Lucifer accepted. "You see, my sister is unequivocally vain and she has particular tastes. She would be very hard to miss."

"Vain, so she'd be pretty," Wyatt surmised.

"Beautiful," Lucifer admitted. "But," he paused.

"But, what?"

"She likes to dress up like little girls," Gabriel blurted.

"When I saw her just before she attacked me, she was in the body of a fourteen-year-old-girl," Lucifer told them.

"Wait," Wyatt said. "She's *possessing* somebody?"

"Of course," Lucifer explained. "How else would demons gain access to the mortal coil?"

"And you're possessing someone right now," Wyatt remembered.

"Well, yes, but to be fair, Tyler here was only for this world a few more days."

"He always picks people who are about to kick it," Gabriel confirmed.

"Wouldn't want to piss Daddy off any more than we have to, would we?" Lucifer smirked. "See, a human body is weak, fragile. When an angel or demon takes up occupancy in one, the power is too great. The body breaks down, cell by cell. Eventually, it's completely destroyed."

"Like radiation poisoning," Gabriel explained.

"Yes, exactly," Lucifer verified. "Now, I have the decency to heal this body intermittently so I don't have to invade another. And, no doubt, my sister will do the same to maintain her attractiveness. The demons, however, are unencumbered by such matters. The longer they inhabit a body, the worse the damage. That's why I do my best to exorcise the intruder as quickly as possible, a job I should be getting back to while we wait for news on the whereabouts of that miserable, treacherous--"

"Okay," Gabriel interrupted. "Before this one gets all worked up and sucks the apartment up into a tornado or something, why don't we talk about something else?"

"What do you suggest, Gabriel?" Lucifer asked, incensed. "I've only been cognizant for a day. The only information I have access to is in this room, and since you're unwilling to discuss *yourself*, that leaves our dear brother. So, what shall it be? Barachiel's whore wife, his indiscriminate genitals, or the fact that he's currently bedding my, what's the term these days? Sloppy seconds."

Wyatt jumped up from his stool and punched Lucifer in the face, nearly knocking him from his seat. Lucifer licked the blood from his lip and grinned.

"That was a warning," Wyatt growled, standing over Lucifer, barely able to hold himself back. "Allydia was a mistake. Mock me all you want for it. I was stupid. But, when it comes to my wife, you *shut the fuck up*. If I even *think* you're about to mention her again, I will *end you*."

Lucifer looked at Gabriel in amazement. "He's really not afraid of me at all. I'm astonished."

"He's not afraid of *anything*," she declared.

"I'm going for a walk," Wyatt announced, grabbing his jacket from the hook and slamming the door behind him.

"You had that coming," she told Lucifer, who raised his eyebrows in agreement, rubbing his jaw. She handed him her cell phone.

"Let me introduce you to a little thing we like to call 'the internet'."

Wyatt walked briskly along the busy street, shoving his hands in his jacket pockets, the autumn air feeling colder as winter approached. As he wandered, from the corner of his eye, he thought he saw someone he recognized. He turned to look, but she was gone. *Strange,* he thought. He stopped at a magazine stand to check the recent headlines. Anything to get his mind off of his altercation with Lucifer. Not the act of punching him; that actually felt really good. But, what he had said, calling Annie a 'whore', did not sit well with Wyatt. No matter what she had done, he still loved her, even if he'd never be able to forgive her. Gabriel had also called his wife names the night before, but it hadn't bothered him, probably because, deep down, those were things he'd been thinking himself. 'Selfish' and 'panicky' just about summed up her actions. If he was being honest with himself, 'whore' didn't seem like that big of a stretch, either, especially since, as far as he knew, she hadn't even filed divorce papers yet.

As his eyes meandered around at the various magazine covers, he suddenly felt an odd sensation. He got chills, the hair on the back of his neck standing up, and it wasn't from the temperature. He turned to look around and saw, several feet away, a man hugging a trash can. He couldn't be sure, but it looked like he was eating the contents. What made it especially odd was that the man was wearing a nice suit and recently shined shoes. Definitely not homeless. As the man stood, Wyatt noticed that chunks of his hair were missing. Large bald spots covered the man's head. He turned around, as if able to feel Wyatt's stare. He looked ashen and sickly, eyes sunken with dark circles underneath. He opened his mouth to reveal holes where teeth used to be. *I'm seeing something weird,* he thought to Gabriel. Just then, the man vomited profusely on the sidewalk. The contents of his stomach were mixed with blood and people walking by scurried away as fast as they could to avoid whatever disease it was they assumed he had.

"Barachiel!" the man hissed in a voice that was not his own. Wyatt was shocked to hear the name. This was it. This had to be a demon. The man bolted down the street, bumping into pedestrians as he went, Wyatt chasing after him. He retreated down an ally as Wyatt followed. Now, he was trapped.

"How are you here?!" the demon screeched. "You're supposed to be in Heaven! I was told we'd have free reign! I was *promised*!"

"Somebody lied," Gabriel said, strolling up behind her brother. The demon made an animal-like shriek as she and Lucifer approached.

"No!" the demon cried. "It can not be!"

Lucifer rushed toward him, gripped him tightly, and threw him up against the fence.

"Where is my sister?" he demanded. "Tell me and I'll do what I can to make this painless."

"I will never tell you, Watch Keeper!" he squawked as Lucifer's hand wrapped around his neck. "She's going to save us from your torment! She's giving us our world back!"

"This world was never yours, you pestilent rubbish," Lucifer insisted. "Are you very sure you don't want to make things easier on yourself?"

The demon cackled. "Lilith will rid you from this place. She will have the humans worshiping at our feet, as it always should have been. And, when Father wakes, after we've exterminated the Earth of all those who oppose us, He'll have no choice but to let us keep this planet. Lilith will have Him bowing to *her*."

"Oh, my," Lucifer guffawed. "You are madder than a March hare, aren't you? You have *met* our Father, yes? What in all of history makes you think that what you're spewing could ever possibly occur? The Almighty would rather crush this world into nothing and start over than to ever bow before *anyone*. He would see us all burn before He would give up a monochrome of power. You forget of whom you speak. *God is all*."

"She is--"

"She is a scourge on this Earth and a pain in my ass," Lucifer proclaimed. "I will find her and when I do, I will not be gentle. As for you, since you've refused to be of any help to me, I'm going to do this slowly." He slammed his hand to the man's chest, a light glowing gradually around it. The demon shook, blood spurting from his mouth, his eyes rolling back in his head. He gasped for breath as what looked like a shadow seemed to peel off of him, slowly falling to the ground, shrinking, and finally disappearing. The man collapsed unconscious to the ground below him, color now returning to his face.

"Jesus," Wyatt said under his breath.

"Where?" Lucifer questioned.

Gabriel laughed. "All right boys, can we please get along better from now on?"

"Seems unlikely," Lucifer told her. "I'm a bit of an ass."

"At least you're self-aware," Wyatt poked.

"See?" Gabriel said. "We're all friends, right? A little bickering between siblings is to be expected. Come on, let's get out of the cold. Oh, yeah, just one sec." She knelt and placed a hand on the man's chest. His skin glowed, white light pouring out of his nose and mouth. His eyes opened wide and he shot up to a sitting position, scurrying away from them to sit up against the fence.

"You okay, buddy?" Gabriel asked.

"What the hell happened?" the man wondered, looking around wildly. "How'd I get here?"

"I don't know," she lied. "We were walking by and saw you lying here. We were about to call an ambulance. You all right?"

The man stood up, visibly shaken. "I think so," he said, patting himself down and feeling his wallet, phone, and keys still in his pockets. He looked at them suspiciously as he checked his wallet, finding the cash and credit cards all still there. He put it back in his jacket and nodded to them as he walked past. "Thank you," he told them as he staggered away.

"Is he gonna be okay?" Wyatt asked.

"He'll be fine," Lucifer assured him. "Our dear sister reversed any damage the possession may have caused. As for the demon, he won't be back."

The three walked back to the apartment in silence, all feeling a sense of accomplishment. No, this wasn't the monster they were after, but it was a start.

Chapter 10

Lilith stopped to admire her reflection in a store window as she made her way back to the theater she currently called home. It was temporary, of course, but she just loved being on a stage, her adoring fans looking on. *Soon,* she thought. *I'll live in the finest palace this world has ever seen.*

While the demons that followed her made attempts to provide her with the food she required, it wasn't enough to keep her satisfied. She had *other* desires.

As she brushed her long blond hair away from her roseate cheek, she noticed a man watching her. She smiled at him and he awkwardly smiled back. She approached him, fluttering her big blue eyes at him as she held his gaze.

"Hi," she said sweetly.

"Hi," he said nervously. "I'm sorry, I shouldn't stare."

"It's not a problem," she told him. "I like to be watched."

The man grew tenser as he sat on a park bench. "I'm just waiting for my bus," he explained.

"I'll wait with you," she cooed. "You know, you're a gorgeous man. Just lovely."

He smiled apprehensively. "How old are you?"

"Not much younger than you, I suspect."

"I doubt that. I'm twenty-two. If you're not at least eighteen--"

"Let's say I'm eighteen."

"Are you?"

She tilted her head and smiled broadly as she delicately touched his cheek. "I can be anything you want me to be," she said, her voice just above a whisper. She leaned in and kissed him, softly at first, and then with passion. *This* is what she had been missing. She quickly reached for his belt, taking him by surprise. He pushed her away.

"What are you doing?!" he asked. "This is a public street!"

"You don't want me?" she barked.

"Not in front of the whole city!"

"You're *ashamed* of me?!"

"What?!" he said, not sure of what the hell was happening. "There are *people*. We could get arres--"

Just then, a twenty-something-year-old-woman on her cell phone walked by and glared at them.

"Is it her?!" Lilith yelled. "Would you rather be with *her*?!"

"Oh, my God!" he shouted, standing up. "Am I being pranked? Is there a hidden camera somewhere?"

Lilith cracked her neck as she stood. "Why did you have to bring *Him* into this?" She grasped the young man's arm and pulled him to a nearby ally. He tried to get away, but couldn't. She was unnaturally strong.

"Stay here," she commanded, using her mind to lift him a few feet above the ground and paralyze him.

"Holy shit!" the man said shakily. "What the fuck?!"

She walked back to the sidewalk in search of the woman. After a few minutes, she found her. She grabbed her by the hair and dragged her on the ground to the ally.

"Is this what you like?" she asked the man, still suspended, forcing the woman up on her knees. She yanked the woman's head back and tore open her shirt, revealing her large breasts.

"Jesus Christ! Stop!" the man begged as the woman cried. Lilith watched angrily as his face grew more and more afraid. She slid her hand down the front of the woman's pants.

"Please," the woman sobbed.

"Don't worry," Lilith said as she fondled her. "It's almost over." She licked the side of the woman's neck and face while maintaining eye contact with the man.

"Leave her alone!" he shouted from above.

"Do you love her?" Lilith wondered.

"What?!" he howled. "I've never met her! You're psycho!"

"You know," Lilith told him. "In my day, youth was prized above all when it came to choosing a woman. These," she said, grasping one of the woman's breasts with her free hand, then gently caressing the nipple. "Were merely icing on the cake."

As her nether regions were being violated, the woman, though she fought the feeling, couldn't help but begin to orgasm. Tears streamed down her face as she came and she cried out in pleasure and torment.

"Why are you doing this?" she whimpered.

"Because, dearest," Lilith replied. "Everyone deserves one last orgasm. My Father's most wonderful creation, wouldn't you agree?" And with that, she whipped her hand out of the woman's pants and plunged it into her chest, tearing her heart from her body in one shocking, violent motion.

"What the fuck are you?!" the man screamed.

She opened his pants and pulled them down along with his underwear. She lightly licked him until he was fully aroused.

"Stop!" he demanded.

She laughed as she slammed him to the cold ground. She swiftly removed her panties and lifted her dress, sitting down on top of him and placing him inside of her. As she rode him, she forced his mouth open and shoved the woman's still warm heart into it. He let out a muffled scream as he looked at the dead woman's body lying in a heap next to him.

"Chew," Lilith told him. He began to cry.

"Chew!" she yelled, using her telekinesis to make his jaw move up and down.

"Yes," she gasped, a feeling of relief washing over her as she climaxed. "Yes! It's so good to be home!"

Chapter 11

"So audition," Valerie said, losing her patience.

"But, what about Corey?" the girl sitting across the desk asked.

"What about him?" Valerie asked, visibly annoyed. "Savannah, you are fifteen years old. Corey is not 'the one', I hate to break the news, and if by some one in a million chance he is, do you really think a couple months apart would be enough to break you up? More importantly, if he's the kind of boy that would hold you back from accomplishing your goals or chasing your dreams, is he worthy of you?"

"I guess not," Savannah admitted.

"Listen, the school can make accommodations if you get through, so you don't need to worry about that. If I were you, with all that talent, *I'd* be at that open call. In my professional opinion, girl, you should be singing."

"What do you know about music, Miss Moore?"

"I know I've been listening to it since before you were born. Now, get out of my office, you know what you want to do."

They both smiled as the girl stood and walked toward the door.

"Thanks, Miss Moore," she said. "I'm gonna go for it."

"Good," Valerie approved. "And have fun. Not everything's life and death."

"Miss Moore," another student said, entering the room, passing Savannah as she left.

"Hey, Javier," Valerie greeted the boy. "Have a seat. What can I help you with?"

The boy sat, face beaming, grinning from ear to ear. "I just wanted to tell you, I got in."

Valerie smiled broadly. "Oh my God, Javier! Congratulations!"

"It's my dream school," he told her. "I'm so excited. And I qualified for all the financial aid I need. I'm going to college and it's all thanks to you, Miss Moore. Thank you."

"Boy, all I did was help you with the paperwork. This is all you. I'm so proud of you."

"Thank you. I gotta get to class. Thanks again."

"Of course. You have a good day."

"You, too." He closed the door behind him and Valerie sighed happily. Javier had struggled to balance school and his job, which he had to keep to help feed his younger siblings. The university he chose was close enough that he could live at home and still work part-time. Valerie was thrilled for him. He deserved this opportunity and she was just grateful to have been of help.

Suddenly, she was startled by loud, incessant knocking on her door.

"Come in," she called.

The door flew open, a woman wearing a bright red sweatshirt with a white turtleneck underneath, faded jeans, and a necklace with wooden stars painted blue dangling from it burst in. She was clearly unhappy.

"Are you Miss Moore, the guidance counselor?" the enraged woman squawked.

Here we go, Valerie thought, doing her best to fake a polite smile.

"Yes," she replied. "How can I help you?"

"I'm Travis Dean's mom," the woman snipped. "You can *help me* by telling my son that you made a huge mistake when you told him to quit football."

"Have a seat, Ms. Dean."

"I will not," the woman said stubbornly. "Call him to your office and *fix this now*."

"I'm not going to do that, Ms. Dean," Valerie told her as calmly as she could. "Travis has been cast in the lead role in the school's production of 'Hamlet', on top of which, he's now the captain of the debate team *and* the Mathletes. He simply does not have time to waste going to practices and sitting on a bench at games. He's just too busy."

"He's a *senior* this year!" Ms. Dean proclaimed. "He'll *finally* get a chance to play!"

"No, he won't," Valerie informed her. "I've spoken to the coach. Travis is terrible. He'll never see the field."

"How dare you?!" Ms. Dean exclaimed. "I'll have your job!"

Valerie stood as the woman turned to leave. "A little advice, Ms. Dean," she said. "Appreciate your son for who he *is*, not for who you *wish* he was."

The woman grunted, storming out in a huff and slamming the door behind her.

After a long day and what felt like an even longer walk home, Valerie finally made it back to her Hell's Kitchen studio. She took off her jacket, letting it fall with a thud to the floor. She kept her keys, wallet, phone, and pocket knife in the massive pockets so she didn't have to carry a purse, making her less of a target for muggers. The neighborhood was pretty safe, but she could never be too careful. The apartment was small, but it was close to school and rent was reasonable. Gabriel had offered to buy her a bigger place, but she had refused. The worst thing in the world for her was feeling like she owed somebody something. She worked hard for everything she had in life and she wouldn't let anyone, not even her sister, take that sense of pride from her.

She put the bag of fast food that would be her dinner on the coffee table, took a fry, and turned on the small television. She watched the evening news intently as she swallowed the french fry and took a sip of soda. Just then, she was startled, her eyes growing wide as she dropped her cup in her lap. She was being gripped by a vision, and it was a doozy.

It was dark, cold, and everything in sight was gray and bleak, seemingly covered in soot and ash. She could hear groans and wailing all around her and the feeling of despair was overwhelming. She could hear voices but wasn't sure where they were coming from. As she searched, noticing the strong stench of sulfur and the stone-like feel of the walls, she came upon two entities. She recognized one of them as Lucifer. She could tell the other was an angel, but she couldn't quite place him.

"The Gates close soon, brother," the angel said. "I'll no longer be able to come for these visits."

"Yes, well, what is a couple of centuries for creatures such as us?" Lucifer quipped.

"I look forward to our next meeting, then."

"See you when Father wakes."

The angel walked toward what looked like a black hole hovering in perfect stillness and turned to wave goodbye. Lucifer waved back and walked off, out of sight. When he was sure Lucifer was gone, the angel quickly turned away from the strange opening in space and instead headed down a darkened corridor. Valerie followed him through a maze of rooms, each containing black, shadowy figures that cried out in anguish as they passed. One contained a twisted, misshapen tree that looked as though it had been carved from lava rock. Another contained a tall, dull-gray obelisk that several of the shadows looked to be attempting to climb. Finally, at the end of the long hallway, the angel came to a locked cell. He looked around anxiously as he ventured to open it. As he struggled, the figure of a woman rushed to the bars. She looked like she was covered in tar, no real face could be made out.

"I'm here, sister," the angel told her. "You'll soon be free once more and while I'm trapped in Heaven, you'll create for us a world in which *we* may rule, as it should be."

After a few moments and a lot of effort, the shackles gave way and the cell door swung open. The woman timidly stepped out, as if in disbelief.

"It's all right," the angel said. "When back on Earth, you can make preparations to keep yourself there as well as Lucifer, should he follow. Come, now."

The two hurriedly sleuthed down the hall, gathering demons as they went, eventually getting back to the black hole, stepping into it, and disappearing, several demons going behind them.

Valerie gasped as she came out of the vision, slowly regaining her faculties. As she calmed her breathing and began to feel normal, she noticed her soda had spilled all over her clothes, the sofa, and the floor.

"Shit," she said.

Valerie pounded on the door, her rage growing as she waited. Wyatt answered, stepping aside to let her in and she passed by without acknowledging him. She stormed through the apartment, making a beeline for Lucifer who sat on the couch reading a newspaper.

"Oh, shit," Gabriel said as she took a chip out of the bag she was holding. She popped it in her mouth and stood next to Wyatt who closed the door and watched as Valerie all but attacked Lucifer. Within seconds, she was on top of him, grabbing the sides of his head with a little more force than was necessary. Lucifer took a shaky breath as he was shown his sister's latest vision. When he had seen it in its entirety, Valerie let him go and stood in front of him, so livid she was nearly shaking.

"You let him in, stupid!" she barked at him.

"That perfidious miscreant!" Lucifer shouted, jumping up, the paper falling to the floor. "I will kill him with my bare hands!"

"You want to fill me in?" Wyatt asked Gabriel.

"Turns out it was Samael that let Lilith out," she told him. "I'm not surprised."

"Who's Samael?"

"Angel of Death."

"Of course."

"Yo, Satan," Gabriel called from across the room. "Angels are taking sabbaticals in Hell now? You get a kickass DJ or something? Put out a spread?"

Lucifer was unamused. "As you may have guessed, Hell can be quite grim. Our brother will, on occasion, pay me a visit. It helps me stay sane."

"Ish," Gabriel joked.

"Yes," Lucifer agreed.

"The fuck were you thinking?!" Valerie demanded. "How could it not occur to you that letting someone like that into Hell might be a bad idea?"

"For context," Gabriel leaned in to tell Wyatt. "Samael can be a little unpredictable."

"Sure," Wyatt acknowledged.

"Do not lecture me, Uriel," Lucifer snapped, moving closer to Valerie and taking an offensive stance as if he were preparing for a fight. "You've seen the torment, felt the agony, the suffering. You've heard the screams of the damned. Imagine constantly existing in that for *millennia*, save the rare trips to Earth once or twice a century where you're tasked with dragging some poor soul right back to it. How would you maintain your identity? Stay vigilant? Remember who you are and whom you serve? You couldn't handle being me for a *day*, so don't you dare berate me for doing what I have to."

"All right, children," Gabriel said, pulling them away from each other with her mind. "Let's not get rowdy. Lucifer, why don't you come with me to get us all some dinner?"

He reluctantly stepped away from Valerie and followed Gabriel out the door.

"I'm really sorry," Gabriel told him as they walked toward the elevator. "I know how miserable it is for you there."

"I appreciate that sister," he said, regaining his composure.

"And Uriel's just--"

"Self-righteous and sanctimonious?" Lucifer interrupted.

"Kind of," Gabriel laughed.

"You okay?" Wyatt asked as he and Valerie sat at the island.

"Fine," she replied, struggling to calm herself.

"So, Hell is--"

"Bad," she confirmed. "Really, really bad."

"Right," Wyatt said. "Hey, you mind if I ask why you pulled a knife on Gabriel? Did she get in your head, too?"

"No," Valerie told him. "She broke into my house."

"Oh," Wyatt chuckled.

"See, when I was fifteen, I was staying with this family. Not the worst place I'd ever lived, but still, pretty rough. I was in foster care cuz my dad killed my mom when I was seven and then he went to jail, right? So, anyway, my foster mom was a junkie and she'd be passing out from too much heroin or whatever at like, nine o'clock every night and it was kind of a bad neighborhood, so I'd be afraid to go to bed, so I'd be up real late just being paranoid. Then, she got this real sketchy boyfriend but it was kind of comforting that there was a big dude in the house to scare off burglars and shit. So, one night, this little white girl comes banging on my bedroom window, telling me to let her in right now. I was like, 'Uh uh, I don't know you', so she broke the fucking window with her elbow and I was like, 'this bitch crazy', so I took my knife out my pocket and told her she needed to get the fuck out my house. About that same time, Russel, the boyfriend, drunk as shit, breaks my door down, yelling about how I should be in bed. So, this itty bitty teenage girl gets between us and tells this giant man to get away from me and says she knows what he's planning. He gets *pissed* and just starts punching her in the face. I run to the living room to get the phone, but Foster Bitch had left it off the charger all day, so it was dead. So, I run back to my room and he's still hitting her, except now he has her pinned up against the wall. I had my knife ready. I was about to stick this motherfucker, but Gabriel puts her hand up to stop me. Then, this crazy bitch starts laughing. Blood's gushing out of her face, her nose is broken, eyes swollen shut and she's *laughing*. So the dude loses it. He throws her down on the bed and tells me not to move. Said he was gonna do her, then me, and I better not tell *anybody*. Then he starts taking his belt off."

"Holy shit," Wyatt muttered, horrified by what he was hearing.

"Next thing I know," she continued. "This asshole goes flying across the room and hits the wall so hard he puts a hole through it. Gabriel looks back at me and tells me to run, but of course, I don't because I'm looking at some science fiction shit right here and I want to see what happens. So, the guy gets up and starts running at her but before he can do anything, she makes this little flip motion with her hand and the dude's head spins around *completely backward*. This bitch just broke this piece of shit's neck with a fucking parlor trick. So, then she goes to the bathroom and washes the blood off her face and she's like, *magically* healed. Eyes back to normal, nose fixed, like *nothing happened*. Then she tells me she found my grandma and she's there to take me to her. I didn't even know I had a living relative. So, at this point, I know this girl is some kind of supernatural *something*, and I'm a little freaked out, but she *did* save my ass, so I figured going with her was better than trying to explain to the cops what just happened. So, I pack my little bit of stuff in my backpack and we take off. I get the keys to foster bitch's car and Gabriel drives us from Camden to Harlem. She tells me who she is, who I am, the whole thing. Says I'll start getting visions when I turn eighteen and that we're gonna be best friends. I'm thinking she's nuts, but maybe she's not wrong. Now, I had never been outside of Jersey, so I wasn't fully believing that we were about to see my long-lost grandma, right? But, we get to this building and before I can stop her, Gabriel knocks on the door. It's past midnight. I was sure somebody was gonna call the cops. But, this old woman answers the door, just as calm as she can be. I tell her what my name is and that I was told she was my grandmother and she breaks down. Turns out, she was my mom's mom and when my mother was in high school, she dropped out to run away with my dad and never spoke to her again. She never even knew I existed. So, we get to talking and she invites me to stay with her, so I moved in. Gabriel stayed with us here and there, but for the most part, it was just me and my grandma until she died."

"I don't even know what to say," Wyatt admitted.

"Yeah, it's kind of fucked up, but it all worked out. Gabriel saved me and gave me my family. She *is* my family. I mean, listen, she's annoying as shit, but I love that bitch."

Chapter 12

While her demons remained nesting in the theater, Lilith had moved on to a suite at a luxury hotel on Fifth Avenue. The towering building with fifty-eight floors and gold embellishments was a much better fit for her current needs. Besides, the kinds of people she needed to aid in her efforts seemed to be quite comfortable there. Room service had prepared a lovely variety of pastries and fruits for her guests that would go untouched until their arrival. She had two meetings scheduled. One with Mitchell Spade, the CEO of Cardinal Rain, a well-known government securities company, and the other with Adam Smith, a cable news and talk radio host with a following greater than she'd had when she ruled Uruk. She had been feeding Adam talking points for weeks, skyrocketing his ratings and propelling him into seemingly overnight superstardom. This would be her first face-to-face with Mitchell, however, and she hoped it would go well. After all, he controlled the largest private military in the world and she'd need those numbers for her plan to run smoothly. Mitchell was the first to arrive.

"Is your mother here?" he asked as Lilith welcomed him inside.

"Well, that's condescending," she replied. "*I'm* Lilith. We spoke on the phone. Danish?"

"No, thank you," he declined, skepticism covering his chiseled, middle-aged face. "I'm sorry, is this some kind of school prank?"

"You continue to insult me as if I *won't* tear your entrails from your body and use them to hang you with."

"All right," he huffed. "That's enough. My time is very valuable."

"As is mine, Mr. Spade," she assured him, gesturing to a laptop on the coffee table next to her. He looked at the screen, dismissively at first, then more carefully.

"Is that," he started.

"One hundred million dollars," she told him. "Ready to be deposited into your private account in the Caymans. All I have to do is press 'enter'."

He studied the page, looking for signs of forgery. There were none. "What is it exactly that you want?"

"I need an army, Mr. Spade. As many men as you can gather. I'm specifically interested in your presence in Iraq."

"I have about eight thousand contractors in Iraq currently but they're--"

"I need ten times that amount," she explained. "To start. The best of the best, heavily armed and ruthless."

"What's the mission?"

"Let's not get ahead of ourselves. To begin with, I require full submission. Your men take orders from *you* and *you* will take orders from *me*."

He chortled. "That's not-"

"You're a mercenary, yes?"

"That's an oversimplification."

"That's *accurate*," she scoffed. "You provide soldiers and I provide money. There's a lot more where this came from."

"How did someone like you acquire that kind of money?"

"You'd be surprised, Mr. Spade, by what people are willing to do for me."

"I can get your men, but I can't agree to *anything* until I know what the mission is."

She slammed the computer closed in annoyance before taking a deep breath to calm herself. "Won't you sit?" she suggested, gesturing toward the sofa behind her. He nodded and they both sat. "There's something I need. Something I need to destroy, actually, in the ruins of the ancient city of Babylon. I can't get to it, however, because, as you know, Iraq has become infested with American military, Iraqi military, terrorist groups. It's one big dust-covered pain in my ass. To do what I need to do, I have to take out everyone in the way. That's a lot of dead warriors. The country's President, I imagine, will be displeased so, while I'm there, I may as well take it over."

"Take what over?" he asked suspiciously.

"Iraq, obviously," she told him. "First. Once we've recruited there, we can expand to nearby countries. Saudi Arabia, of course. Jordan, Syria," a sneaky smile stretched across her lips. "Israel."

"You want to *invade* Iraq, then seize power, for yourself, of the *entire Middle East*?" he guffawed. "You're a child!" he exclaimed, his laughter now uncontrolled.

Angered, Lilith closed her fist slowly in front of her and as she did, Mitchell's chortles turned to gasps as he lost the ability to breathe.

"I'm older than I look," she said through her teeth. The man's skin took on a purplish tint as he suffocated and Lilith debated whether or not she needed this arrogant blowhard. As his eyes bulged and glossed over, she decided he was too useful to kill just yet. She relaxed her hand and he began taking deep, labored breaths. "You're getting off light," she said. "I will not tolerate this insolence in the future."

As he got his bearings, the terror on his face was replaced by awe. "How did you do that?" he asked, his voice scratchy.

"I'm..." she searched for the right word as she stood. "Special."

"I can see."

"Are you in or not?" she pushed.

"What you're proposing is unheard of."

"Only in modern times," she said. "I've done this before. I can do it again."

"I don't understand."

"You don't have to. Can you get the men?"

"I would need some time."

"Not too much, I hope," she threatened.

"I, um-"

"I have a friend, he'll be by later today. I plan, eventually, to ask him for help in sending you recruits. They'll need training and discipline. They will be *in addition* to the one hundred thousand men you hire."

"A hundred thousand?!" he choked, standing in front of her. "I thought you said eighty?"

"Better safe than outnumbered."

"This is impossible, not to mention highly illegal," he told her. "This could trigger World War Three. It would *definitely* piss off the big guy upstairs."

"You let me worry about God."

"Who's talking about God? I meant the Pres-"

"Oh!" she chuckled. " 'Big Guy'. Oh, man. That's funny. But, yeah, fuck him, too." She opened the laptop and slowly typed. "You'll have to excuse me, I'm just learning how to use one of these things." She hit 'enter' and turned the computer to face her new General. "Show yourself out. I need to get ready for my next meeting."

As she sauntered off into the bathroom, Mitchell studied the screen, shocked at what he saw. The girl had deposited ten billion dollars into his account. He pulled his phone from his jacket pocket and called his bank, unable to believe any of what had just happened. After providing passwords and other assurances of his identity, the bank confirmed that ten billion dollars *had* just been deposited.

"Thank you," he said, nearly dropping the phone before he hung up. He let out a long sigh as he regained his composure and headed toward the door. "Time to get to work."

Chapter 13

It had been nearly two months since Michelle's mother had been killed and she still hadn't returned to school. She had somehow managed to keep up with her assignments, but she could barely get out of bed every day. She was sleeping until at least one in the afternoon and staying up at night until she physically couldn't keep her eyes open anymore. Her uncle was letting her get away with it, but she knew she needed to get it together soon. The school had called and emailed multiple times and she had received a letter in the mail stating that if she didn't come in for classes in two weeks' time, she'd be expelled. Her uncle hadn't mentioned it. He was allowing her to grieve as she needed to and she appreciated it. He had been so great, giving her space when she needed it and comfort when she didn't want to be alone. She owed him everything.

As she looked over the letter again, mentally preparing herself to go back, she heard a crash. She opened her bedroom door and slowly walked down the hall. Before she reached the living room, a book went flying past, coming very close to hitting her in the face. She stopped where she was and stayed quiet.

"I thought we could discuss this like civilized adults," she heard Tae say. "But, I guess this is what happens when you date an infant."

"You're calling me childish now?!" a second voice yelled. It was Mr. Marlowe. When he started seeing her uncle, he had told Michelle to call him Harrison outside of school. She couldn't bring herself to do it.

"What would *you* call someone that completely loses their shit if they don't get a text back within two fucking minutes?" Tae retorted.

"It's disrespectful and rude to make me wait!" Harrison griped.

"I was in surgery!" Tae explained for the fourth time.

"So, you were *in surgery* yesterday and three times last week and--"

"Yes, bitch! I'm a *surgeon*. That's my motherfucking job!"

"Now you're being condescending," Harrison said with attitude.

"And you're being needy as shit."

"Needy?!"

"I'm about to start calling you 'dough boy', you're so needy," Tae sassed.

"Well, excuse me for--"

"No, I can't hear it," Tae dismissed. "I don't have room for this kind of bullshit. I'm done. Just go."

"Are you breaking up with me right now?" Harrison whined.

"What was your first clue, genius?" Tae asked. "The 'I'm done' or the 'Just go'?" He impatiently waved him towards the door, but Harrison wasn't having it. He was furious. He picked up the closest thing to him, a lamp from an end table, and before he could stop himself, he raised it, intending to throw it across the room. Instead, he let his fury overtake him and he brought the lamp down onto his now ex-boyfriend's head.

"Uncle!" Michelle screamed from the hall. Harrison hadn't realized she was there. He looked stunned, staring at Tae lying unconscious on the floor. He slowly backed away, guilt and self-preservation setting in. He looked up at the girl's terrified expression. His heart raced and he couldn't think. After a few moments, he turned and darted out of the apartment.

"Uncle!" Michelle yelped again, tears starting to form in her eyes as she watched the pool of blood growing larger on the hardwood floor. She ran to him, kneeling as she cried. She shook him violently, but no response. She checked for a pulse but found none. This couldn't be happening. Not him, too! She sobbed as she rolled him over and slapped his face.

"Wake up!" she commanded. "Uncle, please!"

Tae groaned as he finally began to open his eyes. Michelle let out a sigh of shock and relief.

"Psychotic asshole," he complained, putting his hand to his head. He got up and stumbled to the kitchen sink where he used the sprayer to wash the blood from his head and face. As he dried himself with a dish towel, he noticed his niece staring at him in disbelief. She looked over his head and saw no evidence of what had just happened. There were no wounds.

"How the--"

"Don't worry about it," he ordered, putting the towel on the kitchen counter. "I'm fine. Get me some paper towels so we can clean this mess up."

She ran to the pantry and grabbed a roll of paper towels.

"What--" she started to ask.

"You know my name means 'to endure'," he said, picking up and placing the shards of ceramic and glass in a trash can. "I'm just resilient."

Michelle's hands trembled as she started to soak up the blood.

"Uncle," she insisted. "What *are you*?"

"Fine," he sighed, putting the dustpan and broom down and sitting on the floor in front of her. "But, this stays between us, you hear me?"

She nodded.

"I'm Tae Iha," he began. "Uncle, doctor, life of the party, all that shit. But, I'm also an angel named Raphael that took up occupancy in this body when it was a fetus. I heal myself, I'm really good with directions, but, otherwise, I'm a perfectly normal person. Please don't freak out."

Michelle sat there on the floor, her hands covered in her uncle's blood, shocked and confused by what she just heard. "And, you're not kidding?"

"Not at all."

"Angels are real?"

"Looks like."

"Are there others?"

"Yes, but I am not going to tell you about those people," he said. "They are seven ways to fucked up."

"Have you always known what you are?" she asked.

"No," he told her. "When I was a freshman in college, this girl showed up at my dorm, kicked my roommate out. He was so dense, he thought I was about to get lucky. She told me who I was, said she'd be checking in on me, making sure I was all right, not working too hard. Over the years, she's helped me in a lot of ways."

"She was an angel, too?"

"HBIC."

"So, if angels are real," she asked. "Why didn't one of them save my mom?"

Tae looked sadly at his niece, knowing there was no explanation he could give her that would be good enough.

"It's God's rest time, baby," he said. "It's complicated, I can't go into it. I know it's not fair and it feels like life is just one big heap of bullshit after another and I'm sorry I can't fix it for you. There are only a few angels here right now and they have a metric fuckton of their own shit to deal with. Saving the world type stuff."

"Why aren't you helping them?"

"I did my part," he said. "It's up to them to finish the job. My abilities are no longer needed. Besides, I have other things on my mind. You, work, filing a restraining order."

They both laughed and went back to cleaning. After a few seconds, Michelle's curiosity got the better of her.

"So," she started to ask. "Angels are allowed to be, um--"

"God doesn't give a fuck about our sex lives," he insisted. "Not mine, not yours, not anybody's. Assuming everything's consensual. I mean, from what I hear, there's a special place in Hell for predators."

"I was always told marriage is sacred and people shouldn't--"

"Marriage is *sacred* because two people make a promise to God to love, cherish, blah fucking blah," he explained. "When the preacher says, 'let no one tear asunder', he's talking to the couple. Those two people swore to God that they wouldn't be with anyone else. Breaking that promise is like lying to God, which is a surefire way to piss off the Almighty. But, if you're single, He couldn't care less about who you're sleeping with and he sure as shit doesn't give a fuck if you marry a man or a woman. We're all the same thing to Him."

"How do you know that?" she asked.

"When I was first told about who and what I was, I was scared," Tae admitted. "I thought I was gonna get punished or some shit for being gay. But, she explained it to me and I've been comfortable with myself ever since."

"The angel?"

"Not just any angel," he told her. "The highest authority on Earth. The Messenger of God."

Gabriel quickly put her shirt back on as she looked around for her sock. The woman rolled over in bed, felt that her playmate was no longer there, and opened her eyes. "Going already?" she asked, stretching and then covering her mouth as she yawned.

"Yeah," Gabriel said. "I have to meet my brothers for breakfast. Have you seen my--" she stopped, noticing the woman swinging her sock around in the air. They both smiled as Gabriel took the sock and put it on. The woman sat up and scooted herself behind Gabriel, moving her hair away from her neck then kissing it softly.

"I really have to go," Gabriel said.

"I know," she said, still kissing her.

"Beth,"

"It's Brie," she corrected her.

"Right, sorry," Gabriel apologized. She could hear the thoughts of a man in the apartment above. *Beth is so cool. I hope I get to see her today.* "Listen, I have your number. We'll do this again sometime, yeah?"

"Definitely," Brie agreed.

Gabriel got her shoes on and walked to the bedroom door. "I'll see you later," she promised as she left the room. Brie lay back down to get a little more much-needed sleep.

Gabriel found her coat on the living room floor of the boho-chic apartment and put it on. She checked her pockets for her phone, wallet, and keys and once she was sure they were all in their rightful spots, she exited the apartment, making sure to lock the door as she left. When she got outside, she had to look around to remind herself of where she was. She sighed. Long cab rides home were a drawback of picking up randoms at clubs. She caught a cab, told the driver the cross streets, and pulled her phone out to check her messages. Three texts. From Ethan, *U wanna cum over???* From Lucifer, *I find the programs on your DVR insipid. You should watch more documentaries. Expose yourself to some culture.* And from Allydia, *My man says he thinks Lilith's taken up with a new lover and has headed out of the city. Will keep you posted.*

"Fantastic," she muttered to herself. It had been months since they had exorcised that first demon. Gabriel was getting antsy. She thought Lilith would be back where she belonged by now and she was growing increasingly impatient as time went on. The plan was to lay low until they knew Lilith's exact location and then ambush her, but no one seemed to be able to track her down. Every night, Allydia's goons staked out the theater and, every night, it was filled with the same old demons but no Lilith. She thought about going after the nest because who knew what kind of trouble they were stirring up, but there was no way Lucifer could expel all of those demons at once. Some would get away and alert Lilith that not only was Lucifer awake and hunting her but that there were other angels after her as well. It would blow their cover and without the element of surprise, Lilith was sure to do an even better job of hiding and they might never get a chance to throw her ass back in a cell.

The cabbie pulled up in front of her building and she paid him, including a large tip that would pay for the prescription he'd been putting off getting because it was too expensive.

"Thank you so much!" he told her. "You don't know what a blessing this is for me."

"Yeah, I do," she said as she exited the cab. "Have a good one."

She walked into her apartment, doing her best to be quiet. The boys were still asleep and she didn't feel like having an awkward conversation with Lucifer about where she was all night. She took a quick shower, dried her hair, and put on fresh clothes. She went to the kitchen and opened the fridge to see what was available to make for breakfast. She was starving and it might be nice to make a proper meal for her family for a change. She grabbed a carton of eggs and some butter, then, after placing the items on the counter, got a pan from a lower cabinet and glanced around the room. She was still impressed with how quickly the contractors had gotten the apartment back in functioning condition after Barachiel's meltdown a few months before. The place was stunning. Hopefully, he'd be able to hold it together in the future.

She poured three glasses of orange juice and began to make scrambled eggs. After a few minutes, the pan started to smoke and the fire alarm sounded. She took a newspaper and fanned it until the noise stopped, but it woke the boys up, anyway.

"Everything all right?" Wyatt asked sleepily, taking a seat at the island.

"Fine," she answered. "Just making breakfast."

"What the bloody hell is the racket?" Lucifer called as he came down the hallway.

"She cooked," Wyatt told him.

"She *what*?" he griped. "Do you hate us that much, sister?"

"Shush your mouth," she said, setting plates in front of them.

The eggs were well overcooked and smelled awful. Wyatt took a bite out of politeness but Lucifer covered his nose. "I can't," he told her.

"They are not that bad," she said.

"Barachiel," Lucifer asked. "Thoughts?"

"I don't want to be rude," he said as he struggled to chew.

Gabriel took a bite of her eggs and immediately spit them back out onto her plate. "Okay, they're really gross," she admitted.

"So disgusting," Wyatt agreed, dropping his fork, relieved he didn't have to choke them down.

"This is why I don't cook real food," she lamented. "It's fickle. Toaster pastries never break your heart this way."

Wyatt chuckled as he stood. "If you'll both excuse me, I need to make a call."

"I already handled it," Gabriel told him, taking a sip of her juice.

"Handled what?" he asked suspiciously.

"Your landlord in New Jersey. I called him last week, pretended to be Annie, and paid off your lease. You have about four months before you'll have to renew. You're welcome."

"I don't need you to pay my bills."

"I know you don't," she said. "But, you're not working right now and most of what your uncle left you is tied up in property and you shouldn't be worried about selling houses seven hundred miles away when you're supposed to be focused on fine-tuning your lightning skills. It's unnecessary for you to be stressed out about money when I'm sitting on a stockpile of cash."

"She has a point," Lucifer chimed in.

"Pipe down," Wyatt told him.

"I don't know what your problem is," Gabriel said. "I mean, I do, but it's stupid. I'm just trying to be helpful. It's the sisterly thing to do."

"I don't need yo-"

"My charity, I understand," she sighed. "Ugh, you sound like Uriel."

"How is our lovely sister?" Lucifer asked. "It's been some time since I've seen her."

"That's because she hates you," Wyatt said.

"That's a bit of an overstatement," Lucifer rebuffed. "She just misunderstands me."

"No, she fucking hates you," Gabriel confirmed.

"Well, I'm insulted," Lucifer complained. "I have nothing but respect for our dear Uriel. She's helped me tremendously on dozens of occasions tracking down rogue demons. One incident I remember quite fondly. There was this king in Naples, I'm not sure of the year. It was five centuries ago or so, I believe. Anyhow, he was quite villainous on his own, but then--"

"Yeah," she interrupted. "She doesn't remember that."

"Of course not," Lucifer realized. "Perhaps I should remedy that."

"Don't get crazy," she warned.

"Me?" he said, feigning innocence. "I would never."

Chapter 14

Gabriel had agreed to take Lucifer to see Valerie in an effort to mend their strained relationship, leaving Wyatt alone to work on better controlling his abilities. He had come a long way and was now fairly skilled in keeping his emotions from getting the best of him. He stood on the balcony and watched carefully as he pulled a lightning bolt from the clouds and dragged it across the sky, making sure it didn't come down and hit anything. He felt a twinge of pride as it disappeared into the overcast. Just then, he heard something from the living room behind him. He entered the apartment and closed the glass door behind him, glancing around the room. He saw no one.

"You back?" he called. No answer. From the corner of his eye, he saw someone rush down the hall to where the bedrooms were. Concerned there might be an intruder, he readied a small ball of lightning in his hand as he made his way, finding his bedroom door to be open. He went inside and found a woman standing in the far corner. It was the same woman he'd seen on the street a few months before. She smiled at him and as he got closer and her face became clear, he realized who she was.

"Mom?" he choked out.

"Yes, Wyatt," she said. "It's me."

Wyatt nearly fell over, catching himself on the bed.

"You're," he started, but couldn't finish the sentence.

"Dead, yeah." She slowly approached and sat next to him. He scooted away from her a little as the shock began to wear off.

"And, I'm real, just to be clear," she told him.

He stared, unable to take his eyes off her face. His father had been right. He *did* look just like her. The faded photos from the eighties hadn't done her justice. "I don't know what to say to you," he admitted.

"You don't have to say anything. I just wanted to tell you how proud I am of you. Despite everything you've had to deal with, despite what I did, you've grown up to be such a good man. And I know you're an angel underneath, but to me, you're just my sweet baby boy that I never got a chance to meet. I can't tell you how sorry I am."

Tears filled Wyatt's eyes as all the long-buried pain of his childhood came flooding back. "It's not your fault. You were sick."

"I was. But, I'm okay now and I want to make sure you're okay, too."

"I'm fine," he said, wiping tears from his cheeks.

"Are you?" she prodded. "When was the last time you spoke to your father?"

"It's been a while. It's hard for him."

"Because you remind him of me," she said, tears welling her eyes now, too. "I'll never forgive myself for what I did to you both. John still hasn't recovered. Finding me like that destroyed him. It's my fault. Not his and most certainly not yours."

"He's a grown man," Wyatt said, resentment and anger building as he spoke. "I was a *kid*. A kid with no mother. I deserved better from him. He should have done better."

"You're right," she conceded, letting the tears fall. "He's been a lousy father. But, Wyatt, I *know him*. Before I died, he was a different person. He was so excited when I told him I was pregnant with you. He loved you so much, and he still does, just--"

"Not as much as he loves you," Wyatt told her. "No matter what I did, I was always just a reminder of what he lost. I will never be anything but an emotional burden for that man."

Abigail stared at her son's heartbroken face, crushed by what he'd just said. "I owe you more than I can ever give," she sobbed. "But, I swear, I will fix this for you." And with that, she was gone.

Valerie was enjoying a lazy Saturday. She had some high sugar cereal for breakfast, watched a bad movie on TV, and was still in her pajamas when there was a knock at the door. She ignored it as she scrolled through the guide trying to decide what to watch next. She heard the clicking sound of the door being unlocked, so she turned the television off, jumped up from her seat on the sofa, grabbed a knife from the kitchen, and prepared herself. The door opened and Gabriel and Lucifer came strolling in as if they'd been invited.

"Bitch, what the fuck?!" Valerie yelled.

"You gave me a key for emergencies," Gabriel reminded her.

"Is this an emergency?"

"Not really, but you know how pushy this one can get," she said, gesturing to Lucifer.

"All right, what do you want?" Valerie huffed, setting the knife on the coffee table and sitting back down.

"Is that how you greet guests?" Lucifer asked. "You don't say 'hello', don't offer a beverage? It's really rather rude."

"Lucifer," Gabriel warned.

"Fine, right to it, then," he said. "I just wanted to stop by and make an attempt, even if it proves fruitless, to mend what seems to be broken in our brother/sister relationship."

"Oh, my God," Valerie scoffed. "Are you serious?"

"Quite."

"Listen," Valerie explained. "There's nothing broken, nothing needing mending, okay? I'm not mad at you, I just don't feel comfortable hanging out with the Devil, you understand?"

"Well, that smarts," he admitted. "Might I remind you, sister, of some of our more cordial interactions? Times when we got along well. One might even go as far as to call us friends at certain times in our long history."

"I don't need a lesson in friendship, Lucifer. I'm just trying to have a peaceful--' But before she could finish,

Lucifer grabbed her hand and placed it on his temple. She was immediately inundated with visions. Bits and pieces of Lucifer's memories of her. Most of them were of them hunting and exorcising demons. Others were of them fighting in wars together and of them in Hell, putting the Fallen in cells. When he was satisfied that she'd seen enough, Lucifer released her hand and backed away. She gasped and fell back into the couch, eyes wide, with a look of horror on her face. The feelings of despair from the Fallen combined with the fear and rage of the people and other angels in the wars was overwhelming. As the shock wore off, anger took its place and Valerie snapped. She leaped out of her seat, grasped the knife, and held it to her brother's throat. "I should kill you!" she screamed.

"Take it down a notch," Gabriel interjected, using her telekinesis to pull Lucifer back from Valerie's reach.

"What the fuck was that?!" Valerie yelled. "Why would you show me--" Suddenly, the knife in her hand exploded in flames. She dropped it on the table and it quickly went out without causing any damage. She stared at it in disbelief. "What the--"

Gabriel burst out in uncontrollable laughter. "It's, it's," she said. "It's your flaming sword!" She fell to the floor in hysterics, kicking her legs and pounding the floor with her fist. "Flaming sword!" she cackled again, wiping tears from her eyes. "I can't stand it!"

Lucifer snickered.

"I didn't think you'd ever get this power," Gabriel said, getting herself up off the floor and quieting her laughter.

"You knew about this?" Valerie asked. "Of course you did, look who I'm talking to. The fuck is it?"

"Uriel carries a sword engulfed in Holy Fire into battle," Lucifer explained.

"Apparently, you can access that shit if you get pissed off enough," Gabriel said. "Like B with the lightning."

"It's a good thing our brother wasn't here just then," Lucifer quipped. "His inner firefighter would have kicked into action."

Gabriel chuckled. "Imagine him hosing her down with the sprayer from the sink."

The two laughed while Valerie picked up the knife and returned it to the kitchen. "I need you two assholes to leave now."

"Come now sister," Lucifer said. "I don't like this rift between us."

"I just need a minute to get my shit together, okay?!" she snapped.

"We're going," Gabriel said, pulling Lucifer towards the door. "Relax, have a quiet day off. But, I do want you to make an effort to be less hostile toward our brother."

"Thank you, Gabriel," Lucifer said.

"Bitch," Valerie warned.

"Not today, calm down," Gabriel said. "In the future. Just think about it."

The two left, Valerie closing and locking the door behind them. She sat back down on the couch, propping an elbow up on the arm and resting her head in her hand. She looked around, confused. After a few minutes of quiet contemplation, she muttered to herself, "I need some weed."

"Son of a bitch," Gabriel said as she and Lucifer got back to her apartment.

"What now?" he asked.

"Goddamn ghosts, man," she complained as she headed to Wyatt's room. Lucifer sighed, not at all interested in what that was all about. He made himself comfortable on the couch and picked up the book he'd started reading the day before. It was a gripping tale of organized crime and family. One of the brothers was being ostracized for being different, not as well-liked as his siblings. He could relate.

Gabriel found Wyatt sitting on the edge of his bed weeping. She hurried to sit next to him and held him in her arms, cradling his head while he cried. "It's okay," she whispered, knowing that it wasn't, as she rubbed his back. "It's okay."

Chapter 15

John took one last sip of whisky before heading off to bed. He went around the apartment, turning the lights off and checking that the door was locked. Once in his bedroom, he took his cell phone from his pocket, turned it off, placed it on the charger, and turned to close the door. As he started to unbutton his shirt, he noticed that his phone was now on the floor, not on the bedside table where he'd left it.

"Strange," he muttered to himself as he put it back. As soon as he took his hand away, though, the phone flung itself from the table, back to the floor in the same position as before. *I've had too much to drink,* he thought, rubbing his eyes and shaking his dead. He took his shirt off, untucked his undershirt, and unbuckled his belt, leaving the phone where it was. As he began to unzip his slacks, the bedside lamp, too, suddenly fell over and rolled off the table. John looked around suspiciously.

"Who's there?" he yelled sharply, half expecting to be robbed at gunpoint. No response. "Who the hell's there?!" Still nothing. He went for his phone. "I'm calling the police!"

"And you'll tell them what, exactly?" a voice said quietly from the shadows.

"Who is that?" he shouted into the darkness, panic setting in as he reached for the fallen lamp, the only thing available to use as a weapon.

A form slowly began to manifest as if from thin air. John's heart raced and his breath quickened. He couldn't believe what he was seeing. After several moments, a face became clear and the woman appeared solid.

"Abby?" he marveled, falling to his knees, dropping the lamp and phone, and looking up at the vision of his dead wife.

"Hey, sweetie," she said as she knelt in front of him. John's eyes filled with tears. He tried to touch her face, but his hand went right through her.

"You're a," he uttered. "A ghost?"

"Apparently," she confirmed.

"How are you," he began to ask. "I mean, *why* are you--"

"I came to apologize," she told him. "What I did to you, Johnny is unforgivable. There aren't words for how sorry I am."

"Abigail," he assured her. "I understand. You weren't *you* at the end. *I* should have--"

"There's nothing you could have done," she explained. "I was determined. I would have found a way."

"Why, Abby?" he asked, tears streaming down his face. "Why did you leave me?"

"I was deranged. *Unbalanced*. I thought something terrible would happen if the baby was born and I didn't want to live without him, so in my insanity, I tried to kill us both. I was completely off my rocker. He did nothing wrong, and you certainly weren't at fault, either. It was *all* me."

"I miss you so much," John whimpered. "I miss you every minute of every day."

"I know that," she told him. "But, you have to let me go, John. It's not healthy for you to hold on to me like this. The pictures everywhere, not dating anyone else. The drinking. The drinking, Johnny, is catching up to you. You're not twenty-five anymore. And the way you've treated our son--"

"I know," he admitted. "I know. It's just so hard, Abby. Just looking at him kills me. He's so much like you."

"He's amazing," she said. "I've been watching, here and there. He's so special, John, you have no idea. But, he *needs* his father."

"He's an adult. I don't see a way of changing things between us."

"Find one," she demanded. "*I* know you love him, but *he doesn't.*"

John sprang up in bed, covered in sweat, his breathing heavy. The pale light of the sunrise filled the room allowing him to see his phone and the lamp in their proper places on the nightstand. *It must have been a dream,* he thought. He tried to steady his breathing, but after several moments, he realized he couldn't. He was suddenly overcome with a sense of vertigo, even though he was still sitting in bed. He felt nauseated and weak. Then, an abrupt, excruciating pain filled his chest and radiated down his left arm. Terror gripped him as he clumsily picked up his phone and dialed nine one one.

"Nine one one, what's your emergency?"

John fought to speak, struggling to get even one word out. "Heart," he managed to murmur before dropping the phone, falling back on his pillows, and losing consciousness.

Wyatt woke up still feeling drained from the events of the day before. He had been left reeling after his mother's visit. But, it was a new day and he intended on making the most of it by getting in as much lightning practice as he could. As he threw his blankets off and swung his legs over the side of the bed, he noticed on his nightstand sat a plate with a croissant, a cup of coffee, and a note that read,

It is my sincere hope that this will perk you up before joining the rest of us for the day. As you may have deduced, I'm cheerless enough without also having to endure your melancholy. L

Wyatt laughed a little, putting the note down and taking a bite of his breakfast. He checked his phone. Two missed calls from Tae. Odd. The two had a polite and friendly relationship, but they weren't what one would call close. Until now, the only time Tae had called him was an accidental butt dial. Assuming it must be important, Wyatt called his brother back.

"Wyatt?" Tae answered.

"Yeah, buddy. What's up?"

"Your last name is Sinclair, right?"

"Yeah."

"I thought so," Tae said, slightly embarrassed that he had to check. "You're listed as the emergency contact for a patient that came in a few hours ago. Jonathon Sinclair. From his age, I assume he's your father?"

Wyatt sat up straight. "He is. What happened?"

"He had an acute myocardial infarction. A heart attack. He's stable for now, but I'm keeping him at the hospital for a while. Just thought you should know."

"Jesus Christ, is he gonna be okay?"

"Hard to say," Tae confessed. "I'm keeping a close eye on him, but if you've got anything you want to say, I wouldn't dilly dally."

"All right, thanks, man."

"Mm-hmm."

Wyatt jumped out of bed and threw his clothes on as fast as he could. He took another bite of croissant and chugged the coffee before heading out. "Thanks for the breakfast, Satan," he said as he rushed by Lucifer and Gabriel who were sitting at the island playing chess on his way out the door.

"Is he unaware that I dislike that?" Lucifer asked.

"He knows," Gabriel giggled.

Wyatt hesitantly entered the hospital room where his father was recuperating. He looked fragile and smaller somehow as he lay there sleeping, IVs and monitors flanking the bed. *Nesiritide, Morphine, Saline,* the bags read.

"The good stuff, hey, old man?" Wyatt mumbled as he pulled a chair closer to the bed and took a seat. He wasn't sure what he should do in this situation. He hadn't prepared himself for a moment like this, though he realized he probably should have. His father was in his sixties and while he had appeared to be in good health until now, he drank heavily, worked constantly, and had no semblance of a social life. In hindsight, something like this happening seemed to have been inevitable. Wyatt glanced around the dimly lit room and took note of how cold it felt. The emptiness surrounded him like a breeze as he looked out the small window at the view of another building. Everything about this place felt hollow and impersonal and he wondered if it would aggravate his father to know this might be where he'd spend his final moments. He wondered if he'd care at all about the where and be more concerned with the how or why. And, he wondered if his father's ghost would someday visit him as his mother had or if he'd simply move on, unbothered, leaving this world with no regrets.

John's eyes slowly fluttered open and as he woke he was surprised to see his son sitting there. "Wyatt," he said, his voice scratchy. Wyatt poured a cup of water from the table next to him and carefully handed it to his father. John took a few sips and handed the cup back. "Thank you."

"You okay?" Wyatt asked. "How do you feel?"

"Let's just say, if I had a tail, I wouldn't be wagging it," John quipped.

"Do you need anything?"

"No, I'm fine," he said, trying to sit up and grunting with displeasure when he couldn't. "They shouldn't have bothered you. I'm all right."

"Dad, you had a heart attack."

"Just a little one."

"Dad,"

"Listen, while I've got you here, I'd like to apologize. I know I've been an asshole for the last, well, your whole life, and I want to make sure you know none of that was your fault. I mean, you know that, right? That was *my* bullshit."

"Oh, I know," Wyatt agreed coldly.

"You deserved more from me and I'd like to make it right. Is there anything you need? Money? Advice?"

"Well, if Annie ever gets around to filing divorce papers, I might ask you to go over them for me," Wyatt said, half-joking.

"Done," John chuckled. "She still hasn't filed?"

Wyatt shook his head.

"Huh. Maybe she's not sure."

"It doesn't matter," Wyatt told him. "She's seeing someone. I can't forgive it."

John raised his eyebrows in approval. "Good for you, son. Fidelity is the most important thing in a marriage. If you can't trust your partner,"

"You've got nothing left," Wyatt muttered, looking down at his hands in his lap for a moment, fiddling with the ring he still wore.

"Speaking of wives," John said in an attempt to change the subject. "I saw your mother last night."

"You *saw* her?" Wyatt asked, returning his gaze to his father.

"Well, not *her*, obviously," John corrected himself. "It was a dream or a heart attack-induced hallucination, but it *felt* real. She was as beautiful as I remember and she was wearing the dress I buried her in. She told me I needed to let her go. I don't know if I can. She was *everything*. The sun rose and set with her."

"I know what you mean," Wyatt said, again spinning the ring around his finger. "I can't imagine what it must have been like for you, seeing her, what she did. If I had been in your shoes,"

"You would have done right by your son," John presumed. "You're a better man than me, Wyatt. Stronger. Tougher."

"I don't know about that."

"I do. The things you've been through, having *me* as a father, and on top of that, your mental stuff. I'm amazed you can function at all, but here you are."

"Oh, um," Wyatt said. "I had a procedure. I don't have the hallucinations anymore."

"Really?" John said, sounding pleased. "A procedure? Like, electroshock?"

"Kind of."

"Well, that's great, kid. I'm happy for you. That's the best thing I've heard in a long time. Aside, of course, from 'No, you're not dead'."

As they laughed, a nurse came in carrying a large vase of flowers. "These came for you," she said as she placed it on the window sill and handed John the card.

"Best wishes on your current endeavor. The Rothstein Group," John read allowed then dropped the card on the table next to him. "I should maybe get some real friends."

Wyatt snickered.

"All right, Mr. Sinclair," the nurse said, releasing the brake on his bed. "Time for more tests."

"All right," John conceded. "Listen, Wyatt, go on home. I'm fine. I'll call you if anything changes."

Wyatt looked at the nurse who gave him a reassuring nod.

"Okay," he agreed. "I'll see you later."

"See you later," John said as he was rolled out of the room. "It was nice seeing you."

"You, too, Dad."

That night, after his shower, Wyatt took a good long look at himself in the bathroom mirror. It was time, he decided, that he come to terms with Annie being out of his life. His father wasn't the only one that needed to let a wife go. He looked sadly down at his wedding ring as he hesitantly slipped it off his finger and set it on the marble vanity, making sure it wasn't so close to the sink that it could easily fall in. He cleared the steam that had accumulated on the glass and again looked at his reflection as he applied a layer of shaving cream and picked up a razor. Until now, he had only used clippers to trim down his facial hair, not seeing the value in keeping properly groomed without Annie there to appreciate the effort. It was only about five millimeters of hair, but as he shaved, it felt like years falling away. There was a sense of relief he hadn't expected as he rinsed his face. It had been a long time since he had really *seen* himself and for the first time in months, he recognized the man looking back at him.

Chapter 16

"You've done excellent work, Adam," Lilith said, handing her guest a cup of coffee and sitting next to him on the sofa. "Since our last meeting, your ratings are up even more and you have over six million followers on social media, is that right?"

"Yeah, it's been awesome!" he said in his signature low, excited growl. "People are eating this shit up like ice cream! I'm talking to a guy about making my own line of-"

"That's great, Adam," she interrupted. "Really good news. You've succeeded in getting the people riled up. Enraged. Now it's time for phase two."

"What's phase two?"

She smiled sweetly and slid closer to him. "I need you to create posts on your social media accounts for Cardinal Rain. They're hiring."

"Oh, sure, no problem," he agreed emphatically. "Those guys kick ass! You know, I was in the National Guard back in the eighties."

"That's wonderful, Adam," she condescended. "I also need you to gently *nudge* your followers into taking up arms."

"Oh, my fans are well-armed, trust me. I did a poll a few weeks ago. Almost seventy percent are gun owners."

"Yes, but I need them to *use* those guns."

Adam set his cup down and turned to his benefactor. "What do you mean, use them?"

"Well, they know that big government is out of control," she explained. "They're aware, thanks to you, of the tyranny. The government can't be trusted. Law enforcement, politicians, the courts. It's all the same. Run by a criminal syndicate of elites that want them disarmed and weak so they can control them with indoctrination at public schools, mindless cogs in a--"

"Whoa, whoa, lady," he chuckled. "You know that's just bullshit, right? Stuff I say to provoke people."

"Of course, but your followers don't."

"It's just entertainment," he confessed. "I just say crazy shit people want to hear. It's just for ratings."

"But those ratings translate to real people with real weapons and those weapons now need to be turned on your government officials."

"Are you out of your fucking mind?!" he shouted, jumping up from the couch. "I'm not telling people to *kill* people!"

"It's the next logical step," she said, a little confused that he didn't know this was where things were headed.

"The fuck it is!" he barked. "What I do is *rhetoric*. It's soundbites and slogans short enough to put on a bumper sticker or baseball cap. I don't incite violence."

"Of course you do," she contradicted, standing to look him in the eye. "How many school shootings, pipe bombs, and ass-kickings are you directly responsible for? I've lost count!"

"I'm not responsible for crazy people doing awful things."

"Crazy people that listen to or watch one of your shows. Crazy people that think you're the only person being honest with them because that's what you've convinced them to be true. You are *covered* in the blood of innocent people that your followers deemed unworthy of life. All I'm asking you to do now is direct that energy to the people in charge. Declare the government the enemy of the people. Demand justice. Tell them-"

"Jesus fucking Christ, lady!" he yelled, backing away toward the door. "There is no way in Hell I'm doing that. I'm just an entertainer."

"This is the thing," she said, clearly irked. "If you won't do what I ask, I'll have to start over with someone else. I don't have time for that. People are looking for me. Now, I've done a cloaking spell, but it requires a tremendous amount of energy to maintain. I see no circumstance likely to weaken me occurring any time soon, but you never know. Cardinal

Rain is deliciously close to beginning their mission and I need your government occupied here so they won't interfere with my plans. Now be a good boy and do what you're told." She dropped her hand down hard toward the floor, forcing Adam to his knees. She sat her computer in front of him on the floor and knelt beside him, stroking what little remained of his hair. "Log in to your account."

"No," he insisted.

"Fine," she sighed, rolling her eyes. She took her fist and crushed his hand into the hardwood. He screamed in agony. "Now, login with your left hand."

"I won't," he declared, tears welling in his eyes. "I'm not a monster."

"Pity," she said, standing up and taking a step back. "I am." She clapped her hands, crushing Adam's skull, causing it to cave in on either side. His eyes popped out of their sockets and dangled over his cheeks while blood and brain matter poured from his nose and ears. When his body fell, she kicked it under the bed and picked her phone up off the coffee table. She dialed Mitchell Spade's number as she opened the bedside table's drawer, pulling from it a small limestone box.

"Hello?" Mitchell answered.

"I'm sending you something to make your job easier," she told him. "You may not need it, and you should hope that you don't because using it comes with a price."

"What kind of price?" he asked.

"There are...side effects. It's only in case you come against a resistance you can't handle. Call it insurance. Hold out your hand."

"What?"

She quickly muttered the incantation, the box disappearing from her hand and reappearing in his.

"Holy shit!" he blurted.

"You're welcome," she said, hanging up the phone and dropping it to the blood-soaked floor. "I need a release," she said to herself as she went to the door and left the room, not bothering to close it behind her.

Chapter 17

Tae took off his surgical gown and gloves before washing his hands and heading to his office. He pulled a protein bar and bottle of water from his desk and sat down. He only had about ten minutes to eat while his next patient was being prepped. His late dinner tasted like a bad combination of sawdust and peanut butter, but at least he wouldn't be hungry while he cut into someone. As he guzzled his water, he heard a loud commotion coming from the hall. "What fresh hell?" he muttered as he went to the door and peered outside. At the other end of the long hall, just past the nurse's station, he could see a man flailing wildly as three orderlies tried to strap him to a gurney. He was screaming at them to let him go, blood pouring from his nose and mouth. As Tae got closer, he could see how pale and dull the man's skin was, his eyes sunken with only a few patches of thin hair left on his head.

"What's wrong with him?" one of the orderlies asked another.

"Radiation sickness, looks like," the second attendant answered.

"No way," said the third, struggling to hold the patient down. "By the time symptoms got this bad, he'd be so weak, he'd barely be conscious."

"Holy *shit*," Tae said under his breath.

The man stopped and craned his neck to look at Tae. "Raphael," he hissed.

"Mother f--"

"*Raphael!*" he screeched again, fighting even harder to break free of his restraints.

"Shit, shit, shit, shit," Tae whispered as he scrambled to think of what to do next. He hurried to a locked medicine cabinet, broke the glass, and retrieved a bottle of tranquilizer. He filled a syringe and raced to the gurney, jabbing the needle into the man's neck. The demon squealed and shook before finally passing out.

"Was that necessary?" the nurse asked, gawking at the broken glass on the floor.

"Woman, you have no idea," Tae insisted.

"What's he got?" one of the orderlies asked.

"I--" But, before he could answer, the demon sprang up from the gurney, pushing one orderly to the ground and punching another in the face.

"I'm calling security," the nurse announced as she pressed the alert button.

"Raphael," the demon seethed. "You shouldn't be here."

"Look who's talking," Tae said shakily.

"What are you?" the demon wondered, sniffing the air in Tae's direction. "*Human?*" he gleaned. He cackled, blood and bile spewing up out of his mouth.

Gabriel, I need you at the hospital. You and the Devil. There's a demon. Hurry, Tae thought as the monster ran at him, lifted him over his head, and threw him to the ground. As he tried to stand, he was gripped once more and, this time, dragged from the hall to the stairwell.

"Stop!" Tae could hear a security guard yell. "Stop right there!"

The demon continued, pulling Tae behind him down several flights of stairs. Two security guards followed, shouting and finally letting off a warning shot from one of their pistols. The demon laughed harder at their efforts as he threw Tae down the last few steps. He tried to fight back, but the demon was too strong.

Now in the basement, Tae was heaved up over the monster's shoulder. He kicked and punched to no avail. The demon walked briskly to the hospital's incinerator and opened the door, burning off a layer of skin as he grasped the white-hot handle. The security guards began to shoot, sending bullets into the demon's back and side. It didn't slow him down a bit.

"When you get home," he growled, standing Tae in front of him. "Tell those pharisaic prigs that this world belongs to *us*." And with that, he bashed Tae's head into the hot metal before picking him up, shoving him inside, and slamming the door closed. The security guards were horrified, listening to the doctor's screams until the noise subsided. They continued to shoot, one bullet piercing the demon's heart and another landing between his eyes. He finally fell, laughing maniacally as he was forced out, slithering his way back to Hell, leaving the host body to die.

Gabriel, not willing to wait for Lucifer who was taking a shower, decided to go to the hospital alone. As she reached for the doorknob, she felt the strong sting of Raphael leaving the Earth. She clutched her chest and fell to her knees, unable to breathe, her eyes like saucers. The pain was intolerable. She stared into nothing, a single tear running down her cheek.

"Gabriel," Wyatt called, rushing to where she was, both her hands now on the floor. He knelt in front of her and put his hands on her shoulders. "Gabriel, what's wrong? Are you hurt?"

"I didn't see it coming," she said, her voice just above a whisper.

"Didn't see what coming? Are you all right?"

She looked at her brother's worried face, the concern in his eyes helping her to regain her faculties. He had enough problems. She didn't want to burden him with this until she had to. "I'm fine," she told him. "Something happened."

"What?" he fretted.

They both stood, Gabriel buttoning her coat. "I'll be back."

"Gabriel,"

"I'm okay," she insisted, opening the door and stepping out of the apartment. "Don't follow me."

Gabriel burst through the doors of the old, decrepit theater and strolled in, livid and determined. The building, mostly fallen apart, was crawling with dozens of demons. Some were on the floor and in old broken seats, having sex in seemingly uncomfortable, if not impossible positions. Some were hunched over large amounts of various foods, stuffing their mouths with as much as would fit. One was lying lifeless on the stage, the host's body having given out from being occupied too long. Two others stood over the corpse, splashing it with week-old soda. "Forty days and forty nights!" one of them cackled as the other laughed giddily. Their voices were loud and shrill, like nails on a chalkboard. It grated on Gabriel's nerves as she slammed the doors shut behind her with her mind, using her telekinesis to hold locked all the exits.

"Where's Lilith?" she called to the crowd. They all stopped what they were doing to glare at her in unsettled apprehension.

"Gabriel!" one of them shrieked in horror. Most of them darted for the exits, becoming hysterical when they realized there was no way out. A few brave demons came at her, but she immediately snapped their necks with nothing more than a thought.

"I would tell me if I were you," she warned the rest of them, frustrated that she couldn't decipher their thoughts. Demons' minds were tricky, clouded by the memories of those they inhabited. Nothing came through to her clearly.

"We will never!" someone shouted from the back of the room.

"It's in your best interest," she told them, throwing the two on the stage up into the rafters and bringing them crashing down onto the stage floor.

"No!" several of them shouted in unison.

"I won't ask again," she promised, bringing down a large chandelier, crushing a small group of demons underneath.

"We will not," one of them said, stepping forward, away from the rest as they cowered, blood and bile staining his white tee-shirt, nearly all of his teeth missing. "We have been liberated. Our redeemer *will* rule this place. You are no match. We will not betray she who set us free."

Gabriel sighed and addressed the crowd. "Does this one speak for the rest of you?"

"Yes!" some shouted while others just nodded.

"All right," she said, disappointed. "Don't say I didn't give you a chance." She opened her palms, raising her hands to her sides and as she did, every demon in the building erupted in immense plumes of flame and smoke. They howled as they burned and Gabriel watched, making sure every one of them had fled the body that held them and was sent screaming back to the cages they had come from. When she was satisfied they were all back where they belonged, she hurried out of the building, patting out a small spot at the end of her coat that had caught fire. Not wanting to further damage the historical building, she pulled her phone from her pocket and dialed nine one one.

"Nine one one, what's your emergency?" the operator answered.

"There's a fire," she told the dispatcher. "At the old theater on Canal Street between East Broadway and Grand."

"Is anyone in the building, ma'am?" the woman asked as Gabriel disconnected the call. She looked at the time. One twenty-seven AM. She pulled up another number and began to text.

U up?

There was an immediate response. *Fuck yeah.*

She sighed as she looked at the building, smoke coming from broken windows, the smell of scorched flesh filling the air. She walked the several blocks to Ethan's apartment, unnerved by the quiet stillness that always came after a big snowfall. She avoided stepping in slush or slipping on ice as she went, eventually making her way to her lover's door. He let her inside, gleeful and jittery, like a puppy whose owner just got home from work.

"Hey, sexy," he said as he closed and locked the door behind her. "What's u--"

"No talking," she demanded, quickly removing her clothes.

"You got it!" he complied, tearing his shirt off and pulling his pants down.

She stepped out of her panties and, once naked, walked to the futon which served as the entire living and bedroom in the tiny studio. "Go to town," she told him, lying down.

Ethan kicked his pants away and speedily climbed on top of her. He fervidly kissed her cheeks, neck, and chest, but when he got to her lips, she turned her head dismissively. Not allowing his bruised ego to get in the way of a good time, he again kissed her neck and earlobes, manually servicing her until she became wet. He entered her slowly, moaning with pleasure as he made love to her, knowing, after many past encounters, exactly what she liked. He pulled her legs back, giving her every inch of himself. Her breathing quickened as she became more and more aroused. The night's events melted away with her first orgasm, her mind clearing as her body trembled. *This is why I keep this dude around,* she thought, another wave of euphoria washing over her.

Gabriel returned home to find Lucifer sitting at the island, sipping a cup of tea and reading. She took off her coat, letting it fall to the floor. She opened the pantry and took out a bag of cookies, not bothering to close the door. She sat next to her brother, took a cookie from the bag, and slid the rest over. He took one, studied it, then put it back while Gabriel reached for another.

"Barachiel asleep, then?" she asked, already knowing the answer.

"Yes," he told her. "He tried his best to stay awake until you returned. The poor dear was worried sick. I assured him that you were fully capable of handling yourself and, eventually, he retired to his room."

"But you waited up."

"I wanted to finish my book."

"Right."

The two were silent for a few moments, Gabriel mindlessly eating several more cookies and staring off into space. Lucifer sighed and put down his book. "Do you want to talk about it?"

"Not especially," she replied, gobbling up another cookie and taking a swig of his tea. He raised an eyebrow.

"Come now, sister," he pried. "Tell me what's got you in such a fettle."

She groaned, resting her cheek to her hand. "A demon killed Tae, so Raphael went home and I lost it a little."

"Really?" he asked. "Raphael's back in Heaven?"

She nodded.

"Ah, well. He's in a better place, as they say," he commented, taking a sip of tea. "So," he wondered. "What did you do in your vexation?"

"I *may* have set fifty or so demons on fire, killing the innocent people they were inhabiting and destroying a perfectly good, albeit abandoned and run-down theater in the process and then banged some dude for three hours trying to forget about it," she confessed, taking another bite of cookie.

"Well," he said, both eyebrows raised now. "Seems like a perfectly reasonable response to me."

"Does it?" she asked, not convinced.

"Of course. I wouldn't beat myself up too hard if I were you. For the most part, as far as I can tell, you're taking your current predicament in stride."

"Which predicament?" she scoffed. "Not being any closer to finding Lilith, becoming a mass murderer, or making myself sick on sugar at four in the morning like a drunk teenager?"

"I was speaking of your humanity, Gabriel," he explained. "Uriel shudders with fear at the sight of me. Raphael was concerned with matters that were inconsequential at best, and Barachiel is a roller coaster of emotion and inner turmoil, but *you* remain steadfast in your duties, just like me. You haven't given up on finding Lilith, no matter how difficult it's been. So, you killed a few people letting off a little steam, who hasn't? Those humans were probably too far gone to be saved, anyway, and you needed to deal with your situation the best way you could. I, myself, indulge in the occasional fit of rage followed by long depressive episodes of solitude and reflection. At the end of the day, God's will is done, and that's what matters. If it makes you feel any better, had I developed a bond with the human version of our dearly departed brother, I would have slaughtered those people as well."

"It really doesn't," she smirked.

"What?" he mocked. "Knowing that you're just like *the Devil* isn't a comfort to you?"

She snickered as she got up, threw the empty cookie package in the trash, got a bottle of water from the fridge, and headed to bed. "Night," she called from the hall.

"Good night." Lucifer rinsed his cup in the sink and walked to the living room. He decided to catch up on world events by watching a few minutes of early morning news before going to bed himself.

"The grisly murders have law enforcement perplexed," the reporter read from her teleprompter. "All forty-one residents of the Delta Nu Phi sorority house at Burgoyne College in Schenectady were found late last night with their faces disfigured and their hearts removed. One witness said he heard screaming from the fraternity house across the street, prompting him to call for help, but did not enter the sorority himself for fear that someone may have a gun. The school had recently held active shooter drills where students were instructed *not* to engage an assailant under any circumstances. Classes have been canceled for the week and--"

Lucifer turned the television off, anger rising in his chest as he placed the remote gently on the ottoman. "This is *her* doing," he said to himself. He peered down the hall to make sure Gabriel hadn't heard. Once he was sure he wouldn't be followed, he carefully made his way to the door, being as quiet as he could as he opened it. He stepped out into the hall, locking up behind him. As he got in the elevator, a wicked smile crept across his face as he whispered to himself, "Field trip."

Chapter 18

Allydia looked on as Lucifer fled the building, no doubt going after Lilith himself after seeing the news of his twin's latest exploits. She doubted he'd find her, though. Lilith had proven impossible to track down, even for Allydia's most skilled hunters. She began to worry that her step-mother knew she was no longer the ally she once was. If so, she was no longer safe in the city and may need a change of scenery.

She flew up the side of the apartment building and snuck noiselessly in through Wyatt's bedroom window. She admired him fondly as he slept. Even when unconscious, he wore a pained expression. It wasn't surprising. She had been watching, taking note of his schedule, studying every move while she perched atop the building across the street. She had kept her distance, not trusting that she wouldn't hurt him again. But, this night, she could no longer control herself. She was enamored with him. Everything about him captivated her. From the way he wielded his power, moving lightning through the sky, to his general disposition; pensive and short-tempered. She found his indignation irresistible, his umbrage stimulating her sensibilities in a way no man before had ever been able to. He was *perfection* and after months of holding herself back, she *would* have him again.

She stood over him and brushed the hair away from his eyes. She delicately touched his face, beginning just above his eyebrow and sliding her fingers down, first to his temple and then down to his cheek. He woke with a start, grasping her wrist, a light electrical charge transferring from his hand to her. This only excited her more.

"Easy. I won't bite," she said seductively, pulling her arm away. "Well, I'll do my best."

"What are you doing here?" he asked, still half asleep.

"You know why I'm here," she said, removing her coat and dress with supernatural speed, throwing his blankets back, and climbing on top of him.

"Allydia," he admonished.

"Yes?" she cooed. As she moved her lips closer to his, the overwhelming sense of longing and serenity that had taken hold of him before returned, his will to refuse her fading.

"Last time we did this, we almost killed each other," he reminded her.

"I know, but was it not worth it?" she asked, gently nibbling on his lower lip and stroking his cheek. "I don't know if I like this," she told him, inspecting his skin, now visible after having been cleanly shaven.

"My face?" he asked, feigning offense.

"My father told me never to trust a man without a beard."

"My father told me never to trust *anyone*."

"That's not bad advice," she told him, taking his hand and placing it on the small of her back. "Touch me," she whispered, leaning in closer and kissing him softly. She slid her hand from his neck to his shoulder and as his arousal became apparent, she slipped him smoothly inside her, both of them letting out quiet sighs of pleasure. He took hold of her legs, pulling them apart even further and squeezing her thighs as she writhed, months of pent-up frustration finally being released. Within only a few minutes, she was already beginning to orgasm. In the dim light of the busy street several floors down that illuminated the room through the still open window, Wyatt could see Allydia's teeth starting to grow. He flipped her on her back and took her throat in his hand, holding her down on the bed while being sure not to squeeze too hard on her neck.

She gasped and smiled with delight as he took charge.

"No teeth," he grunted as he continued thrusting.

"As you wish," she breathed, watching intently at his changing face. The intensity of her orgasm triggered Wyatt's own frenzied climax, both of them struggling not to cry out in ecstasy for fear of being discovered. When they had finished, he removed his hand from her throat and looked into her eyes.

"Did I hurt you?" he asked.

"No," she assured him, touching his chin ever so gently with the tips of her fingers. "I honestly don't think you could." He lay down next to her, catching his breath. She looked again at the handsome man she now shared a bed with, and for the first time in millennia, she felt what she thought she remembered to be happiness. "I have to go," she told him, slithering out of bed and back into her dress. He sat up, noticing the time.

"The sun'll be up soon."

"Yes," she said, buttoning her long coat and throwing the hood up.

"So, is it like in the movies?" he wondered. "If sunlight hits you, would you burst into flames?"

She laughed a little. "No. I'm merely sensitive to the sun's radiation. It weakens and exhausts me. My children, however,"

"Your children?"

"Yes," she explained. "Every vampire in existence was either sired by me or by one that I sired. I'm the first of my kind, the strongest and most powerful. The sun, on its own, can't kill me. But, the others are more susceptible. Exposure to ultraviolet light for even a few seconds can," she paused. "Have you ever seen a hot dog being microwaved?"

"Ouch," he chuckled.

"Indeed."

"Hey, can I ask, why are you helping us? Gabriel said Lilith's your step-mother. Why do you hate her?"

"A long time ago, she took something that didn't belong to her," she explained. She went back to the window and sat on the sill. "Until next time."

She was gone, moving so quickly that it seemed as if she had disappeared into thin air. In her absence, Wyatt's mind cleared. He let out a long, disillusioned sigh and he rubbed his face in self-disapproval. "I'm an idiot."

The bodies had been cleared, but copious amounts of blood remained. It covered everything; the floors, the walls, the furniture. "Why would she do this?" Lucifer asked himself, peering suspiciously around the grim scene. The sorority house was dark, only a little light from the rising sun peeking through the curtained windows, which were also splattered with gore. "Her motivation for rampant violence is typically jealousy, but, why would she be--" And then it occurred to him. The quoted witness from the news had been lying.

He left the house and headed swiftly across the street. From the sidewalk, he could see through the windows that every light in the place was on. These boys had no doubt been shaken. He pounded on the door impatiently, a nervous-looking young man eventually answering.

"We already told the cops," he said, his voice trembling. "We didn't see nothin'."

"Well, hello to you, too," Lucifer greeted, glancing past the boy and taking note of several young men whose expressions ranged from terrified to ashamed. "I'm not with the police department."

"Like I said,"

"I know about the girl," he stated.

The man's face dropped and the house fell silent. "What," he stammered. "What girl?"

"Oh, I'm sure you know the one," Lucifer taunted. "Blond hair, wildly insecure. Underage."

The young man looked over his shoulder at his friends who pleaded with him with their eyes. "Look, man, I didn't know she was, I mean, she looked kinda young, but," he stopped and looked back again.

"It's all right, son," Lucifer told him. "You boys aren't in any trouble. The truth is, my colleagues and I have been looking for her for months. She's what you might call *special*."

"Like, some secret government experiment type of shit, right?" someone from inside shouted.

"Something like that," Lucifer said. "It would be very helpful if you could tell me what happened here tonight."

"Okay, listen," the first man said. "If I tell you, do you *swear* to keep it on the DL? We can't have this crazy shit getting out on the news. Our lives would be *trashed*."

"My word is my bond," Lucifer promised.

"All right," he said, stepping out onto the porch and closing the door behind him. "I don't wanna talk about it in front of them. A lot of 'em are really fucked up over it."

"Of course."

The man looked around to make sure no one was in earshot before he started. "Okay," he began. "So, my buddy, Mark, brought this girl back to the house and took her to his room. Now, I was *sure* she had to be a high school girl, but you can't tell Mark nothin', and she didn't look wasted or anything, so I figured she was into it. About twenty minutes go by and we hear Mark screamin'. Not like, *good* screamin', you know what I mean? Like, he was *hurt*. So, I get to the bottom of the stairs cuz I'm gonna go check it out. What if he accidentally choked the girl too hard or somethin', right? But, before I get up there, the girl comes out, completely naked, askin' if any of us know who Sydney is. Now, I know Sydney's Mark's ride or die, but I'm not gonna say shit cuz that's my boy. But, one of the new guys pipes in, sayin' she lives across the street like she's gonna hop on *his* dick for ratting Mark out or some shit. So, she comes down the stairs and asks me if Sydney's prettier than her. Now, I have *four* sisters and if there's one thing I know for sure, it's that if a girl with crazy eyes asks if some other chick is hotter, the answer is always '*hell* no', so that's what I said. That must've made her happy, cuz she grabs me, drags my ass to the couch by my shirt, yanks down my pants like they're nothin', and starts ridin' me right there in front of everyone. It was a little weird, but you take it where you can get it, yeah? Next thing I know, me, Brayden, and my boy, J Dog are runnin' a train on this girl, and it's kinda fucked up, but I'm not havin' a bad time. After a while, though, I start hearing the guys on the other side of the room and they're yellin', freakin' out, straight up cryin' if I'm being honest with you. I look over and they're all buck-ass naked and doin' stuff, like, with *each other*. Dudes sayin' shit like, 'I'm sorry, I can't stop.' while they're giving it to some guy up the ass. Weird oral shit happening everywhere. And, no joke, the Freshman that ratted Mark out was pinned to the fuckin' ceiling, jerkin' it, jizzin' all over people. He was stuck up there by some kind of voodoo, bro, I'm not playin'. I see all this and I can't help but yell, 'What the fuck?' because I mean, what the fuck?! And the girl starts laughing like it's the funniest shit she's ever seen, gets up, puts on somebody's shirt she got off the floor, and leaves. Everybody stops fuckin' and the kid drops from the ceiling and lands flat on his fuckin' face, dick still in his hand. Nobody says shit. We just put our clothes back on and help the kid up, lookin' at each other like 'What the fuck just happened?' At this point, we hear Mark, still upstairs screamin' his fuckin' head off. So, me and Brayden go up there and he's tied to the bed, naked, and both his legs from the knee down are turned *completely backwards*. Bone's stickin' out and shit. So, we run over, get him untied, and asked him what the fuck happened. He points to his phone and there's a text from his girl asking if he's comin' over later. He says the girl saw it and asked who Sydney was. He tried to play it off, but the girl wasn't havin' it. She broke his legs with her bare hands. So, Brayden and J took him to the hospital and when I was helpin' get him in the car, I start hearing girls screamin' from across the way. No way I'm goin' over there after what just happened. No freakin' way. So I call the cops and tell 'em I hear girls screamin', but that's all I know. Cops show up and tell me all those girls are dead. *Dead.* I didn't tell 'em about the chick cuz it sounds crazy, right? Who's gonna believe that freaky shit? I'd end up in the loony bin and my boys would never forgive me for letting that shit out. They don't want people knowing about, *you know.*"

"Yes," Lucifer acknowledged, a little taken aback by his sister's latest shenanigans. "You boys have reputations to uphold, I'm sure. Do you happen to know where she went? See in which direction she headed?"

"No, man, sorry. You think she's gonna come back?"

"I wouldn't worry. She tends to leave carnage in her wake, but she rarely returns to the scene of her crimes. She gets bored quite easily."

"So, what is she?" the young man wondered. "Witch? Alien? Mutant freak?"

"She's much worse than that. The likelihood of her making another appearance is slim, but if you should see her again, I suggest you run."

"No doubt, no doubt."

As Lucifer walked away, the man opened the door to go back inside. "Stop cryin', Cody!" he could hear someone shout from inside the house. Lucifer chuckled a bit as he headed back to the street where he found Gabriel waiting for him.

"I thought you were asleep, Gabriel."

"I find it amusing that you think I'd just ignore you sneaking out," she said.

"Yes, well, did you at least find anything useful while you were spying on me?"

"No," she admitted. "Security guard, groundskeeper, a couple of kids. None of them saw anything. I searched all over. She's long gone. Also, your sister's *fucked up*, bro."

"Does that surprise you?"

"No, but, I mean, she's *really* fucked up," she emphasized. "Like, she needs *massive* amounts of therapy. A team of specialists couldn't wrangle the army of cuckoo going on in her head. The girl has more issues than National Geographic. Crueler than a Congressman taking health care from kids."

"Are you quite finished?" Lucifer asked, annoyed that Lilith had slipped through his fingers yet again.

"Nuttier than squirrel--"

"Yes, she's unapologetically mad. Severely insane. I understand."

"Out of her tree," she joked. "Round the bend. Unzipped."

"Yes, yes."

"Flippity flop banana pants."

"What?"

"So unhinged, no one knows where the door went."

"All right!"

"Just one more," she promised. "Battier than the underside of a haunted bridge."

"All right, that one was pretty funny."

The two returned home a few hours later after stopping for pancakes and coffee. Wyatt emerged from his room just as Gabriel was setting out three plates and unpacking the carryout. "Oh, dude!" she said, exasperated. "*Again*? Now I'm gonna have nightmares."

"Can you turn that off?" Wyatt asked, irritated. "Do you *always* have to be in my head?"

"It's involuntary," she said.

"What has our little brother done this time?" Lucifer inquired.

"Dia," she told him.

"Really?" Wyatt griped.

"What? It's not like *he* can judge."

"Don't worry, Barachiel," Lucifer said. "I won't ridicule you for your lack of judgement. I know all too well the hypnotic seduction of Allydia Cain. It's preternatural. Not much you can do if she has you in her sights."

"Can we please not talk about this?" Wyatt pleaded, taking a cup of coffee from the drink carrier.

"Okay," Gabriel said. "You want to hear about Lilith's latest?"

"You know where she is?"

"No, but we sure as shit know where she was last night."

"What'd she do?"

Gabriel swallowed a bite of pancake before answering. "She killed a bunch of sorority girls and incited a forced orgy at a frat house." She gobbled up the rest of her breakfast while Wyatt stood in astonishment. "Oh, and she broke some dude's legs, but that's kind of low on the list as far as horrific shit goes, you know, comparatively." She stood, kicked off her shoes, leaving them on the kitchen floor, and headed to her room. "I'm taking a shower and a nap," she announced. "Can you fill him in?"

"Happy to," Lucifer agreed.

"What the hell, man?"

"You should sit down."

Chapter 19

Later that afternoon, Gabriel called Valerie over for a family meeting. She was reluctant to go, having stayed away as much as possible in an attempt to avoid Lucifer. But, her sister said it was important, so she went, telling herself it was only for a little while and that as soon as she heard whatever this big news was, she was out.

The four siblings gathered around the kitchen island, Wyatt and Valerie on one side, Gabriel and Lucifer on the other. The tension was high as Gabriel tried to find the right words, knowing that Wyatt would probably be fine, but no matter how she put it, she was about to break Valerie's heart. She and Tae had always been close and the news of his death was going to crush her. Gabriel cleared her throat and took a breath before starting. "Last night, Tae called to me, saying there was a demon at the hospital. He asked that we, Lucifer and I, come help. Lucifer was in the shower, so I decided to go on my own."

"Shit, girl, you okay?" Valerie asked.

"Yeah, I'm fine," she told her.

"Oh, God," Wyatt muttered, realizing what must have happened. "That's when you fell."

She nodded, keeping her eyes on her sister. "As I was leaving, I could feel him. He left."

"What do you mean, 'he left'?" Valerie snapped.

"He's not here anymore," she said. "He went home, to Heaven. So,"

"You're telling me Tae's *dead*?!" Valerie asked.

"Yeah."

"How is that possible?" she questioned. "We're fucking *self-healing*. The only way is if--" she stopped, horrified at the thought of how he must have died. "Fire?!"

"I'm gonna spare you the details," Gabriel said.

"You're gonna *spare* me?!" Valerie erupted in anger. "How the fuck did we not know this was gonna happen? Why didn't I get a vision ahead of time?"

"I don't know," Gabriel answered stoically, a phrase she didn't utter often.

"How do you not know?" Valerie shot back. "You know goddamn *everything.*"

"Not everything," she corrected, starting to get irritated by Valerie's thoughts. She blamed her for Tae's death, angry that she didn't somehow prevent it from happening. Gabriel tried to keep a cool head, but after the events of the night before, her nerves were pretty much fried.

"Clearly," Lucifer chimed in.

"Dude," Wyatt warned him.

"What?" Lucifer asked as Valerie began to sob uncontrollably, Wyatt rubbing her back to try to comfort her. "I'm just pointing out the obvious. Our sister, in her current form, is not at full power. Had she been--"

"Had I been," Gabriel interrupted, her annoyance turning to anger. "You would still be in a coma until I handled this Lilith thing myself because I wouldn't need you."

"That may very well be true, sister, but as it stands, we're one angel down and no closer to finding my malfeasant twin. I can only hope we find and defeat her before the rest of you get picked off."

"I'm doing my best, okay?!" Gabriel barked. "Between Barachiel's meltdowns, your general douchebaggery, Tae ghosting for months, and Uriel's open disdain for you and your bullshit, I've been doing *everything* to keep this family together, civil, and on task. *None* of you make it easy. You think I'm not pissed off that Lilith's still out there? I'm *livid.*"

"You're *seriously* thinking about the *mission* right now?" Valerie complained. "Our brother just died!"

"Our mission from *God* to save the human race from indentured servitude to a psychotic, baby-eating whore-monster? *That* mission?" Gabriel howled. "Hell yes, I'm thinking about that. I'm *always* thinking about that and if there's ever a minute in the fucking day when you're *not* thinking about it, then maybe I haven't made it clear to you just how fucking important it is. It is the *only reason* we're on this planet instead of in Paradise, which, by the way, is where our brother is right now, so you'll have to excuse me if I'm not blubbering like a toddler that got the wrong color sippy cup. There's work to do, and until it's done and that bitch is in a fucking cell, *nothing else matters.* Your job, your social life, your issues, and your motherfucking feelings are just gonna have to take a back seat!" Gabriel calmed herself as the others sat silently, not sure what to say. Her outburst had shocked them as none of them had ever seen her get agitated. "I'm sorry I yelled," she said, getting up from her seat and getting a bottle of water from the fridge.

"I gotta get out of here," Valerie said, wiping the tears from her cheeks and nearly knocking the stool over as she stood. She blew past Gabriel who let her go, not making eye contact. She slammed the door behind her, leaving Gabriel to lock it back.

"I could've handled that better," she recognized. She sat back down and took a sip of water.

"My 'meltdowns'?" Wyatt asked.

"You cry a *lot*, bro," Gabriel told him. He raised an eyebrow while Lucifer chuckled.

"Well," Lucifer said. "I, for one, am quite inspired by what you said, Gabriel. I'm proud of you for standing up for yourself and impressing on everyone the gravity of--"

She cut him off. "Just shut the fuck up."

Valerie was a little more than halfway home when she was suddenly struck with a vision that was so strong and clear that it knocked her to her knees right there on the sidewalk. She saw a building that she recognized as the women's clinic almost directly across the street from where she was. Inside, she could see a handful of people, some slumped in their seats or on the floor in the waiting room and others behind the counter, all dead, their necks broken. There was someone in the back, in a storage room far away from the offices and

exam rooms. All she could see was a doctor lying in the
hallway, blood pouring from his head, his eyes open and
vacant. The door was cracked and there was light coming
through, but she couldn't see who was inside. It didn't matter,
though. Valerie could guess based on the level of evil she felt
coming from that room.

"Miss, are you all right?" she heard a man ask as she
came out of the vision. He was kneeling in front of her, one
hand on her shoulder.

"I'm okay," she told him as they both stood.

"You sure?" the man asked.

"Yeah, I'm good. Low blood sugar, that's all."

"Okay, okay," he said, reaching in his pocket, pulling
out a business card, and handing it to her. "Well, listen, I have
to get to a job right now, but that last number is my personal
cell. Maybe you could call me sometime and let me feed you."

The card read *Malik Perry, Private Chef and Culinary
Instructor.*

She looked back up at him, just noticing how attractive
he was. Tall and muscular with a shaved head, strong jawline,
and wide smile.

"I'll do that," she flirted as he walked away and she put
the card in her pocket. Once he disappeared into the crowd of
pedestrians, she looked across the busy street to the clinic.
"What are you thinkin', ho?" she whispered to herself as she
began walking toward it, navigating through traffic, paying no
attention to the crosswalk just a few feet away. She knew she
wasn't thinking clearly, still reeling from the news of her
brother's death. Even more than that, though, Gabriel losing
her temper had thrown her for a loop. She'd never seen her
like that. It had startled her, the look in her eyes downright
frightening. Valerie knew she couldn't handle Lilith on her
own, but she was *right there* and if she could save the people
inside, convince them there was a bomb threat or gas leak so
they'd evacuate *before* Lilith got there, she had to do it. Then,
she'd call on Gabriel to gather the troops and wait for the
bitch to show up. That was her plan. But, she was too late. As
she entered the dimly lit building, she was sickened by what

she saw. As it had been in her vision, everyone in the clinic was dead.

"Holy shit," she uttered under her breath.

"Uriel?" a voice called from the back. "What are you doing here?" A young girl came out from the shadows of the hallway and into the waiting room looking genuinely confused. Her hands, mouth, and chin were covered in blood as was the collar of the long white dress she was wearing.

"Lilith?" Valerie asked, her voice not much louder than a whisper as she was horrified by the realization of what she'd just walked in on.

"It's amazing," Lilith said, licking her fingers. "Entire facilities dedicated to the legalized murder of tiny humans before they've been born. Can you imagine? And people called *me* a monster just for finding them delicious."

Valerie edged toward the glass door that she'd come in, knowing she was no match for someone as strong as Lilith, not by a long shot. As her back touched the handle, she heard the door lock behind her. Her heart began to race and her mind swirled, unable to string a plan together, knowing there was nothing she could do.

"Was it you?" Lilith asked as she approached. "Did you kill my subordinates? Seems so unlike you, destroying all the so-called innocent people my followers were populating, but it *has* been a couple thousand years. People change."

"I didn't kill anybody," she replied, her fear turning to anger as she thought about the demon that killed her brother and how he was only there because of her, the psycho that now threatened to take her own life. She let the pain of her loss fuel her rage, believing it was her only chance of getting out of this alive.

"No," Lilith said. "I didn't think so."

"But, I'd have no problem putting your little girl wearing ass down."

"Well, that's hostile."

"I'm about to *show you* hostile, bitch!"

Lilith came closer, the look of bewilderment returning to her face.

"Even at full power, which you're obviously not, you don't stand a chance against me alone, and you *know that*. So, I ask you again, *what are you doing here?*"

Valerie shakily pulled her knife from her pocket and held it to her enemy's throat.

Lilith giggled. "You can't be serious."

"I'm dead fucking serious, bitch."

"Have it your way," Lilith sighed, waving her hand, throwing Valerie into a wall across the room. She slammed against it and crashed to the floor. She struggled to stand back up as Lilith moved toward her again. "If you didn't kill the demons in the theater," she gathered. "Then, someone else did. Who else is here? It can't be Michael, he'd never leave Father unguarded during his sleep. Is it Camael? I thought I felt his presence a few weeks ago, but it's been so long, I could have been mistaken." She grabbed Valerie by the throat and slammed her into some chairs. She climbed on top of her, squeezing with one hand her cheeks and chin while she decided what to do with her. "This is quite a beautiful body you've chosen, sister," she said, looking Valerie over. "Tell me, is incest still as taboo as it was in the beginning? So many things have changed."

Valerie panicked, adrenaline coursing through her veins. She started to hyperventilate, which only excited Lilith more. She slid her hand down from Valerie's jaw to her chest and began unzipping her jacket, a mischievous smile creeping across her face. As Lilith slipped her hand inside the jacket, running her hand along Valerie's left breast, the knife, which remained clenched in Valerie's hand, erupted in flame. Without hesitation, she plunged the fiery pocket knife into the monster's gut, again and again, lighting her dress on fire. Lilith flew back into the wall behind her, screaming in pain and surprise. She patted the fire out and fell to her knees, coughing up blood and trembling.

Lilith's psychic hold kept the door locked, so Valerie kicked the glass until it shattered, allowing her to squeeze through and make her escape. She ran and kept running all the way to her apartment where she collapsed on the floor, completely out of breath and terrified. She took her phone from her pocket and texted Wyatt, not wanting to get a lecture about not calling on Gabriel sooner.

Lilith's at the abortion clinic on Broadway. I'm pretty sure I hurt her real bad with my fire-knife.

After a few seconds, she got a reply. *Gabriel and Lucifer are literally cheering.*

Are you sure she's still there? she heard Gabriel ask.

Bitch, I don't know, she replied. *I took off. I'm not trying to die today.*

Chapter 20

The three siblings rushed to the clinic only to find it swarming with police and EMTs. Lilith was long gone, but they got a glimpse inside at the carnage she'd left behind. The scene was grim as body after body was loaded into the coroner's van.

"She knows we're here," Gabriel told her brothers. "If we don't find her before she heals, we're fucked."

"I'd like to say she can't have gotten far with her injuries," Lucifer said. "But, I don't feel her *anywhere*."

"She's hiding out *somewhere*," Gabriel said. "B, why don't you check out the theater. It's a long shot, but anything's possible. Lu--" she turned to look at Lucifer, but he was gone. "Fucking shit."

Wyatt entered the old theater, carefully making his way through every room and corridor, being as quiet as he could be. After about an hour of investigating, he was sure the place, smelling of char and decay, was empty. As an ex-firefighter, he recognized the lingering smell of burned flesh and knew something terrible had recently happened there. The main theater room was covered in soot, a lot of the wood having been burned away. Broken glass littered the floor, still wet from the fire department's efforts. Wyatt wondered what had gone on. Did Lilith kill her own minions? To hear Lucifer and Gabriel tell it, she was capable of anything. Did they set each other on fire? Was it an accident? Were demons even the ones that died here? No other clues remained, save a fast-food cup lying on the stage. He looked around one more time, his curiosity piqued, as he opened the door to leave.

"I'm sorry," Gabriel said, walking into her sister's apartment.

"Girl, for what?" Valerie asked. "I understand. After seeing that bitch in action, I get why you're all about the mission at hand."

"I shouldn't have yelled at you," Gabriel admitted. "Lucifer, sure, but you didn't deserve that. I should have been kinder, considering."

"Well, probably, but that's not really who you are, is it?"

"No, I guess not."

The two sat on the couch, Gabriel knowing what her sister was wondering about. "It was me."

Valerie stared at her, eyes wide. "What the--"

"I know," she said. "I know. If I had waited, brought Lucifer, maybe we could have saved those people. *Maybe*. But I was not in a good headspace."

"You crazy bitch," Valerie muttered. "You *killed* those people."

"Yeah," she said pensively. "But, when Tae died, Uri, I *never* felt like that before. I've never been upset like that."

"You've never been upset before?" Valerie condescended.

"I've never been *sad* before. Not really."

"Now I know you're lying. Your parents died when you were *fifteen*."

"I meant what I said," Gabriel insisted. The two sat quietly for a moment before Gabriel spoke again. "I didn't tell you everything about Tae's death."

"I know," she said, visibly miffed.

"When I said I felt him leave, that's not the whole story. I didn't just feel Raphael's absence. I felt *Tae die*. I *felt* him being burned alive. I *felt* his pain and his fear. I *felt* him suffocate. I heard him *begging me* to save him. And, I couldn't. I *couldn't*. So, I went looking for Lilith because I wanted to kill her with my bare hands. I wanted to wrap my fingers around her throat and watch the life drain from her eyes and I wanted to see her true form so I could burn it until there was nothing left. And, when those demons wouldn't tell me where she was, I lost it. I burned them all. I stayed in that room, choking on smoke until I was *sure* they were all back in cages and the worst part of it is that I don't feel bad about it *at all*. If I had to do it over, I'm not sure I wouldn't do the exact same thing because at least those things are off the streets and back where they belong." Tears filled Valerie's eyes, Gabriel putting a comforting hand on her knee. "I know that I don't usually let my emotions get the best of me," she said. "I don't typically *have* many emotions if I'm being honest. *Gabriel* is always reasonable. Always in control and level-headed. Doesn't get attached. But, *Taran Murphy* loves her family. You, Barachiel, Raphael, even Lucifer. The mission takes precedence because it *has to*, but you guys, you're *everything* to me."

Valerie wiped away her tears, considering everything she'd just heard. She thought for a while then sighed. "That's really deep and I feel like you need a hug," she told Gabriel. "But, *Taran Murphy* needs to get her shit together because *Valerie Moore* isn't gonna hang out if you're out there slaughtering people."

"I'll try to control myself."

"Try hard, bitch. I got enough stress without worrying about you, too." Valerie said, hugging her sister. She would forgive her for now, understanding her mindset at the time, she herself having gone a little homicidal on Lilith not an hour before. But, she'd be keeping a close eye.

Wyatt gathered the energy from the air around him to form balls of lightning, throwing them, one after another at the targets he'd set up on the roof a few months before. He hit one bullseye and then another, over and over, growing more confident in his ability to fight Lilith with every shot. He turned his eyes to the clouds, using his anger and grief to summon a thunderbolt and bring it down hard into the rubber mark. As it struck the target, Gabriel and Valerie were thrown back, having just walked onto the roof to find him.

"Oh, my God! Are you okay?!" Wyatt called. "I didn't see you."

"Show off," Gabriel joked as she helped her sister up.

"Are you all right?" he asked, hurrying to Valerie's side.

"Yeah, I'm good," she told him. "So, you and the vampire a thing now?"

"Come on! Why is everyone so concerned about who I'm sleeping with? I don't ask about *your* private life."

"If I had one, I'd share that shit voluntarily," Valerie scoffed. "I'd be so happy, I wouldn't be able to keep it to myself. Listen, I'm no expert, but according to every sitcom I've ever seen, talking about who we're fuckin' is just something family does."

Wyatt sighed. "No judgement?" he asked. Both women nodded. "It's like I can't control it," he admitted. "Like a fog comes over me and I *have* to--"

"That's vampire shit," Gabriel explained. "She, more than any of them, has like, a pheromone thing happening that makes her irresistible to men. The closer she gets to you, the stronger it is."

"Succubus," Wyatt said, remembering that Allydia had said she'd been called that in the past.

"Yeah," Gabriel confirmed.

"So, I'm getting roofied?"

"No, I mean, you don't lose free will," Gabriel said. "You're not getting knocked out, just a little impaired. It's kind of like she slips you ecstasy. You know what you're doing and you could stop if you wanted to, but you *really* won't want to."

"That's fucked up."

"Vampires, man," she shrugged.

"Did you find Lucifer?" he asked.

"No," Gabriel answered, obviously annoyed. "He went looking for Lilith. He hasn't found her, so now he's blowing off a little steam."

Chapter 21

"What can I get you?" the bartender asked sweetly as Lucifer sat down at the half-empty bar.

"A bottle of your strongest beer, and keep them coming."

"The one with the highest ABV that I've got is fifty dollars a bottle. You still want it?"

Lucifer pulled the credit card Gabriel had given him from his pocket and put it on the shiny marble counter. "Do your worst," he told her, smiling charmingly. She smiled back as she retrieved the bottle from under the bar and opened it for him, pouring him a glass.

"Thank you, love," he said, taking a sip.

"London accent?" she inquired.

"It would seem so."

"So, how long are you in town?"

"Hopefully not that much longer," he told her. "I have a little business to take care of before I return home, although I admit, I'm not exactly looking forward to the trip."

"Afraid of flying?"

"No, it's just that the place I call 'home' is," he thought for a moment. "Lonely. Dismal. *Ghastly*."

"Really? I've always wanted to visit the UK. So much history. Big Ben, the Tower of London, the Globe Theater. Seems romantic."

"It *can* be."

"How long have you been away?"

"From London?" Lucifer asked, trying to recall the year. "It was fifteen eighty-two, I believe."

"That long?" the girl chuckled.

"It's been quite some time."

She giggled, leaning forward, allowing him to see nearly halfway down her shirt. Lucifer noticed her attempts to flirt with him and he encouraged them. He continued to smile and held eye contact and she pushed her long, wavy, dark hair behind her ear. She put her elbow on the bar and rested her tawny cheek on her hand. Her big brown eyes and full coral lips had certainly gotten Lucifer's attention. He shouldn't let himself be distracted by this beauty. He needed to find his sister while she was still weakened, but this woman's cleavage seemed to be beckoning him and the truth was, one of the only good things about being trapped in a human body was the chance to indulge in the pleasures of the flesh.

"I'm Mariana," she told him.

"That's lovely. You can call me 'Lou'. Would you like to hear a story, Mariana?" he asked.

"Sure," she said emphatically.

"As I'm sure you're aware, this bar has stood since eighteen ninety-two and has changed very little over the years. However, in nineteen twenty, the federal government passed the Volstead Act, outlawing the sale or manufacture of alcoholic beverages, except for religious purposes. Of course, the law was never much enforced in New York, but when it was first enacted, bar owners were terrified of being put out of business, so they found creative ways of keeping their doors open. Instead of selling drinks, one might receive a free beer with the purchase of a bowl of peanuts that just happened to cost the same price as a beer had before Prohibition. Others ignored the law outright for fear of rioting. Most required a code word either for entry or to buy the forbidden products. As it became harder to acquire the alcohol needed to satiate the masses, bar owners resorted to bootleggers to meet demand, giving rise to organized crime. One night, one such bootlegger had become dissatisfied with the terms of the agreement he'd made with the owner of this particular establishment. He refused to deliver the goods that had already been paid for. Patrons lashed out, breaking glasses and screaming obscenities. Until a man, we'll call him 'Lewis', explained to the crowd that it was the seller, not the proprietor, that was to blame for the shortage. He then led the mob to the home of the bootlegger where they proceeded to *persuade him* to reconsider. By night's end, the bar was stocked once more and customers developed a loyalty to the place, feeling a sense of ownership for helping in keeping it afloat."

"What happened to the bootlegger?" she asked.

"He was fine after a short stint in the hospital. I'm sure he got what was coming to him, though."

"Miss!" an older man called from the end of the bar.

"Don't you move," she said as she walked off to attend to her customer.

"Wouldn't dream of it," Lucifer said, taking another sip of beer. He glanced around the room, impressed with how well it had been maintained. For a moment, he felt as if he were back in that time, rallying drunkards instead of on the hunt for his malevolent sister.

As his new conquest tended to other patrons, Lucifer thought about the last time he had visited Earth. Elvis was on the radio and there was a hydrogen bomb panic, giving rise to a bomb shelter industry whose underground bunkers would have been all but useless had an attack actually happened. It was in one such bunker that he had tracked the demon he'd been searching for. It had taken over the body of a little girl, about four years old, a crime Lucifer would not see go unpunished.

"Please!" the demon had squealed when he'd been found, cowering in the corner of the shelter. "Let me be!"

"You know that isn't possible," Lucifer had told him.

"I'll kill the girl!" he'd hissed, holding a fork to the child's throat. Lucifer rushed over, grasping the fork and flinging it to the floor. He placed his hand on the girl's chest, making quick work of the exorcism, enraged at the gall of the demon. To possess any human was forbidden, but to possess a child was superior in its repugnance. Once back in Hell, he'd be sure to reprimand the monster considerably.

The demon had taken its leave, Lucifer left holding the little girl as she struggled quietly to breathe. She was in bad shape, unable even to open her eyes, and wouldn't make it, even if he could get her to a hospital. He wasn't very practiced in healing and wasn't sure he could save her, but he knew his

Father would be angered at the loss of this child to such circumstances as these, so he gave it a shot.

He placed his hands on the girl, one on her head and the other on her chest, and concentrated. Slowly, her skin began to glow and the damage the possession had done started to diminish. She opened her eyes with a start, jumping up and backing away.

"You're all right, now," he'd told her, feeling a little disoriented. Healing another while maintaining his own host body's integrity had taken a lot out of him. The girl looked at him, remembering everything that had happened to her over the last few days. She walked back to where Lucifer still knelt on the cement floor, threw her arms around his neck, and hugged him tightly.

"Thank you," she said quietly.

Lucifer gently hugged her back, surprised at how touched he felt by the girl's gesture. "You're very welcome," he'd told her.

She ran off, up the stairs, and out into the yard of the small Midwestern home. "Mommy, mommy, mommy!" she'd yelled. A woman stepped out onto the porch and fell to her knees at the sight of her daughter who, after days of looking progressively sicker with no diagnosis from the doctor, seemed to be her usual, healthy, happy self. The girl leaped into her mother's arms and the two held each other for several seconds. Tears of joy streamed down the woman's face as she looked up and saw Lucifer exiting the bomb shelter. He'd waved as he walked away, wanting to take the body he was in as far away from the family as possible before leaving it. No reason to traumatize them further.

As he sat at the bar, he wondered what had become of that little girl. Then, he remembered he had access to all the known knowledge of the world on the phone Gabriel had given him. He took it from his pocket and tapped on the button that brought up the internet. He typed in the girl's name and the state where he'd left her. Three people came up in the results, but only one was the right age. He clicked her profile and was pleased to find she was still living, a grandmother of four, and a retired social worker.

"Friend of yours?" Mariana asked, pouring him another beer as she'd noticed his glass looking dangerously close to being empty.

"You might say that," he said, putting the phone away.

"I'm jealous," she quipped. "So, what's your business? Must be important for you to come all this way."

"It is. I'm a headhunter of sorts. I've been tasked with finding a particular woman with a specific skill set. My boss insisted a long time ago that she be brought into the company, lest she take her abilities elsewhere."

"I see. And, from the look on your face when you talk about her, she's giving you a hard time?"

"You have no idea."

Just then, a group of men burst through the doors, laughing and talking very loudly. They sat at a nearby table and one of them called to Mariana, "Yo, can we get some whisky?"

She sighed softly as she placed four glasses on a tray, filled them, and walked them over. Lucifer watched as two of the men stared as she made her way back behind the bar while the others sucked their drinks down so fast, it was like they were trying to win a race. These were the exact kind of humans Lucifer tried to avoid. Brash, rude, and utterly uncivilized, seemingly missing the use of the higher functioning parts of their brains. The misogyny wafted like the scent of manure from the table, Lucifer able to hear the vulgar comments they whispered about the bartender. He was already feeling frustrated, doing his best to hold back from violence, and these sorry excuses for the masculine gender were testing his resolve by their mere existence.

"Well," Mariana said, continuing their conversation. "I'm sure you'll track her down. You don't strike me as the kind of guy to give up easily."

"Your instincts would be correct. I'm the epitome of conviction when it comes to my work." His eyes twinkled as the two flirted. He found her very attractive, with high cheekbones, rich olive skin, and just a hint of a Latin accent he couldn't quite place. Her beauty plus the beginnings of inebriation were a welcome distraction from his duties, which he knew he needed to get back to, just not quite yet.

"Baby!" one of the men shouted. "We need another round!"

"Be right back," she told Lucifer seductively as she got the order together and rushed it to the table. As she placed the glasses in front of the men, one of them brushed her leg. She pulled back quickly and gave him a look of warning.

"You got great tits," he said.

"This isn't that kind of place, guys," she told them.

"What kind of place?" one of the other men asked.

"Enjoy your drinks," she said, turning to walk away.

"Hey!" the first man shouted, grabbing her arm. "When a man pays you a compliment, you say 'thank you'." He pulled her closer, trying to sit her on his lap. She fought her way free only for him to grasp her arm again.

"Excuse me, love," Lucifer said, stepping between Mariana and the table. "Could you freshen my drink? I'm feeling a bit peckish."

She nodded and hurried back to the bar, relieved to put some distance between her and the men. Once she was safely behind the counter, Lucifer turned his attention to the table.

"Mind your fucking business, fa--" But, before the abuser could finish his sentence, he was met with a swift punch to the face. Lucifer hit him again, this time breaking his cheekbone and knocking him unconscious. The others appeared shocked as Lucifer went calmly back to his seat and took a sip of beer as if nothing had happened. They dragged their friend out of the building, shouting obscenities as they went, Lucifer smirking and trying not to laugh.

"Sorry for the ugliness, pet," he told Mariana. "Those cretins were being disrespectful and, to be honest, in my head, I'd already laid claim to you."

She looked at him hungrily, impressed and turned on by his defense of her. "Follow me," she commanded.

She led him to a storage room, pushing a pallet of boxes in front of the door to act as a makeshift lock. She kissed him hard, reaching under her skirt to slip off her panties. He held her face in his hands as they kissed and she unbuckled his belt and unzipped his pants. He lifted her onto a crate of pickled eggs and pulled his pants down, letting them fall to his ankles. She pulled him closer and ran her fingers over his manhood, subtly checking it for anything that felt like it could be an STD. When she found nothing out of the ordinary, she spread her legs wide, inviting him in. He accepted her proposal, sliding himself inside her and beginning the act he'd been denied the last sixty years.

"I only have a few minutes," she breathed, grabbing his posterior with both hands, urging him to go faster. "No one's watching the bar."

He touched her cheek again, looking into her eyes with determination and longing. "Your exquisite loveliness has captivated and beguiled me," he told her. "No offense to your work or this establishment, but they'll both have to wait. I plan on relishing you."

He kissed her neck as she moaned with pleasure, her eyes rolling back. She wrapped her legs around him and ran her fingers through his short, wavy hair. In her rapture, she decided getting fired would be well worth this highly satisfying experience.

Lucifer left the bar with Mariana's phone number written on a napkin securely in his pocket. He didn't know if he'd ever see her again, but it was nice to know that she would be available should he require her company in the near future. The sun had begun to set and it was quite dim in the alley, but he could very clearly make out the group of men from earlier there waiting for him.

"Isn't this a little cliche', boys?" he sighed as one of them started toward him. The man raised his fist, but Lucifer grasped it with his left hand, crushing several bones, causing him to cry out in pain. This angered his friends, all of them rushing to attack Lucifer at once. They tried and failed to lay hands on him. The four of them were no match for God's most powerful angel.

Lucifer beat them bloody, throwing one into the brick wall of the building next door, bashing the back of his skull in. As they fought, the anger and frustration of not being able to find Lilith bubbled over, the rage overwhelming him and, soon, he had lost all control. He noticed the man that had treated Mariana so inappropriately trying to flee. His fury was too strong and, before he knew it, Lucifer had taken the man by the hair and pulled his head savagely from his body.

As he looked around at the scene he had created, all four men dead, blood and gore everywhere, the madness slowly subsided. He didn't want Mariana finding this mess, becoming traumatized, and blaming him, so he stuffed all of the bodies, and their severed parts, into a nearby dumpster, took a lighter from his pocket, ignited the flame, and threw it in. The flames weren't as high as he would have liked, but with the small amounts of alcohol coating much of the garbage's contents acting as an accelerant, he was confident the fire would do the job. He hurried off, making sure there was no one around who would have seen what happened.

On to the next adventure, he thought.

Chapter 22

He walked for a long time, trying to calm the rage that had taken over, and he was almost feeling better until he heard it. The ravings of a zealot.

He followed the voice until he came upon a man handing out pamphlets and yelling at passersby. His words were the rantings of a fanatic, and most everyone on the busy street ignored him completely.

"Homosexuality is a *sin!*" the man shouted. "These politicians trying to *normalize* behavior that's *clearly* the work of the *Devil* are putting your children at risk of *eternal damnation!* This is the inevitable outcome of *decades* of going against *God*, ignoring the Scripture, and doing whatever feels good! First, it was interracial marriage, which is *clearly forbidden* in Genesis 28:1 and Leviticus 19:19. Then, it was allowing women to work instead of staying home with their babies as *God intended*, Titus 2:5. Then, gay marriage, Leviticus 18 and 20. Now, we have these freaks calling themselves *trans*. These abominations are--"

"Excuse me," Lucifer said, approaching the man, his anger growing. "You do realize that fanatics like you are the reason that people have turned their backs on God in higher numbers than ever before, yes?"

The man was visibly offended. "I'm trying to *save* people from the eternal Hellfire of the--"

"What you're doing," Lucifer interrupted again. "Is confusing your own bigotry with religion. Genesis 28:1 describes a conversation between Jacob and Isaac in which the latter warns the former not to marry a Canaanite because of the politics of the time. It had nothing to do with race and it's absurd to think that The Almighty would be at all interested, much less angered, by people with different skin tones marrying. That you honestly believe that God concerns himself with who you are or are not sleeping with is more tragic than your choice in trousers. Titus was an all right fellow, but a bit of a misogynist and *Leviticus*," he scoffed. "I'll just say that to call it nonsensical rubbish would be a kindness."

"*God said--*"

"You have no idea what God did or didn't say," Lucifer corrected. "I, however, was there for all of it. Let me enlighten you."

As the man opened his mouth to speak, Lucifer snapped his fingers, rendering the man paralyzed and silent. While his eyes frantically looked around for help, his captor continued.

"First," he began. "Race is just a set of genetic markers having to do with where your ancestors evolved. It has no bearing on your worthiness or ability or *anything*, really. Aside from looking ever so slightly different and a few health considerations, you are *all the same*. If you weren't, would you be able to breed? Can a dog and a cat make hybrid offspring? Of course not. But, an Asian and an African can produce beautiful children. More importantly, God doesn't give two shits about what you all look like. Your bodies are nothing but carts to carry your souls around in for a short period of time. Now, you may come from different countries and cultures, but those are human-made variations that, again, God doesn't care about.

As for homosexuality, it's nothing new. God decided when He created you that to prevent overpopulation, a certain percentage of you would be attracted to the same sex, just like most other creatures on Earth. We all thought it was quite genius at the time.

And, as for *allowing* women to work, or do anything else, for that matter, here's a newsflash for the misogynist in you: women are men's *equals*. Do I need to say that again? *Equal*. The reason men sought to oppress the females of your species was that my sister inflicted such unimaginable horrors on the earliest humans that they became paranoid beyond reason. Women decided to stay with their children while the men would go hunting because they feared, rightly so, for their safety. Over time, men's fear of Lilith became fear of women and that fear turned to anger, which led to a feeling of superiority. They turned their wives and daughters into servants and viewed them as a burden. They were considered the property of their closest male relative. In some cultures, they still are. The western world likes to think of itself as more inclusive and feminist than it once was, and for the most part, that's true. But, then, there are vile creatures like you. You, who wish to enslave your women and make second-class citizens out of entire groups of people. And based on what? Skin color? Sexuality? Gender? You're a buffoon. And you have the *gall* to assume you know what God wants? You're *oblivious* to His wishes. Do you know what infuriates my Father more than anything? Do you? Of course, you don't. I'll tell you. Misunderstanding. Specifically, misunderstanding that leads to disrespect, cruelty, or pain. Systemic racism, bigotry, sexism, with xenophobia being the most ridiculous since none of your religions have ever gotten it exactly right." He stepped closer, speaking directly into his ear. "From my perspective, it seems as though some of you just aren't happy unless you can look down on someone else. You're disgusting and barbaric, spewing rubbish and infecting the feeble-minded with your hateful disinformation. It's people like you, vile and contemptible, that keep your boot on the necks of those you call 'different' that are the real monsters of this world."

He glanced down at the man's hand and saw a wedding ring. "Well, that's horrifying," he determined. "I'm going to do the poor woman that chained herself to you a favor." He backed away from the man, far enough that people walking by wouldn't connect them. He held up his right hand and slowly made a fist. As he did so, the man began to quiver, then shake violently as he stood there on the sidewalk, still unable to move from that spot. Blood poured from his mouth, nose, and ears. Pedestrians screamed and several people called nine one one.

Lucifer smirked as he happily watched the man die, his internal organs crushed to the point of near liquefaction. When he was satisfied of the bigot's demise, he released his grip and allowed his body to fall to the cold concrete below.

The pamphlets the man had been holding were now scattered and blowing around on the pavement. Curious, Lucifer picked one up.

Wife talking back? Children sexually confused? Need help? Come learn how you can take back control of your family and put God back in their hearts.

Lucifer took note of the address and checked his phone for the time. "Better hurry," he said to himself. "Wouldn't want to be late."

Lucifer strolled casually into the church, irritated by what he saw there. Signs on the wall that read, *'Take back your God-given rights as the head of your household'* and *'Condemn the wickedness of the homosexual culture'.* The pews were full of middle-aged white men, all eager for the arrival of the dead man, hoping to be taught how to better control their families. Lucifer, instead, stood at the pulpit, being sure to leave the doors open to the street.

"Well, well, well," he addressed the crowd. "There's not a decent person among you, is there?"

The men muttered, confused and angry.

"Don't be so sensitive," Lucifer said. "I'm just acknowledging what you must already know. You're all trash. You've come here searching for a way to gain respect from your wives and children, but the truth is, and you know it to be true, that they don't respect you because you don't *deserve* respect. Let me ask you all a question. Have any of you ever tried just not being a dick? Just to see what it's like?"

"What the hell is this?!" a man yelled from the back. "I didn't come here for a lecture."

"Of course not. I'll get to the point shortly. But, first, I'd like to share a secret with you. Not a *secret,* really, more like a misconception. Hellhounds. Does anyone here know what those are?"

A man in the front row raised his hand.

"Yes," Lucifer called. "The man in the red hat."

"Giant monster dogs from Hell?" he guessed.

"So close, but no," Lucifer corrected. "That's the myth. See, over millennia, things get distorted, exaggerated. Men who shapeshift into wolves become giant wolf-men. Deer with a single horn become unicorns. And, an obedient worker with anger issues becomes the source of all evil. I'll be honest with you, that last one stings. Anyhow, the true story of the Hellhound is that the Devil, as you like to say, can control anything in nature. Plants, the weather, the sea. He can cause earthquakes, tidal waves, and volcanic eruptions. And, he can control and bend to his will all animals, including dogs. Dogs are his favorite because they can be the most precious, sweet-tempered, and loyal creatures on Earth, or the most vicious and deadly, depending on their mood. I can relate to that. So, when the Devil is particularly agitated, he likes to enlist dogs as his personal murder machines."

Another man raised his hand.

"Yes, a question." Lucifer nodded toward him.

"Look, man," he said. "I don't know what kind of preacher you are, but when are we gonna talk about how to get our women in line and turn our queer sons straight again?"

The crowd cheered. Lucifer was incensed and decided to move things along. "A question for the group," he began. "Who do you think God will be more upset with? You ignorant, abhorrent experiments in wickedness, or me, the dutiful, but admittedly quick to bouts of violence son who massacred the lot of you?"

They looked at him and each other, dumbfounded and enraged.

"I suppose we'll find out in a couple hundred years or so," he said, raising his fingers to his lips and whistling loudly. As he placed his hand back down on the lectern, dozens of dogs of various breeds rushed in through the open doors. Some stray, some with their collars and leashes still on, all wild-eyed and bearing their teeth. They growled and barked as the parishioners panicked, trying to run for the doors, but being held back by the ferocious canines.

Lucifer couldn't help but laugh as he watched the beasts attack, tearing flesh from bone, ripping out throats, and biting off noses and fingers. Two of them, attached by a double leash, worked together to pull out and feast on the intestines of a man who was not yet dead. Blood and gore covered every inch of the room, a mess of limbs and unrecognizable body parts littering the floor and seats like garbage after a concert.

When his appetite for butchery was satiated, Lucifer walked calmly through the carnage, admiring the beauty and strength of the hounds, still chewing hungrily on what was left of the malicious fiends. He whistled again as he left the building, the dogs wandering out behind him, their usual dispositions returning.

The events of the evening, while enjoyable, did little to alleviate Lucifer's frustration. He knew that however he chose to distract himself, he would remain irate until he put his sister back in a cell. On the long walk home, he realized something else. Gabriel was going to be pissed.

Allydia watched from the roof of a building across the street as Wyatt walked from the kitchen to the living room sofa, giving his sisters bottles of water while they discussed strategy. She could hear them talking. They had scoured the city and were running out of ideas as to where Lilith could be hiding. She, herself, had men posted all over town with strict instruction to call her if they see any evidence of her whereabouts. So far, they'd come up empty.

She gazed fondly at Wyatt as he spoke to Gabriel and Uriel, occasionally brushing a rogue strand of hair away from his eye. She was completely captivated. So much so that she didn't bother turning her head when she felt Lucifer walk up behind her.

"It's a little unbecoming, don't you think?" he asked.

"Lucifer," she greeted him, still not facing him as he stood next to her.

"You must explain this to me. What is it about Barachiel that you find so interesting?"

"Nothing," she told him. "It's *Wyatt* that intrigues me. He's fascinating."

"Ah, the human persona my dear brother is currently chained to. Tell me, is it the personal baggage, the emotional instability, or the tendency to cry at the drop of a hat that gets your nether regions tingling?"

"It's his eyes, I think," she said, still watching through the windows. "And his intensity. He's all rage and despair. It's intoxicating."

"Well, that's unhinged."

"I would call it 'passionate'."

"And, I would call it stalking, but potato, potahto. Just don't let Gabriel see you. She's developed somewhat of a maternal instinct when it comes to our younger brother. If she knew you were camped out here, observing him like a zoo animal, she would be less than thrilled."

"I don't answer to your sister," she said firmly.

"Don't you?"

"Speaking of, how is Gabriel going to feel about all the people you killed tonight? I can smell their blood all over you. Lucky for you, I've already eaten."

"Yes," he said. "She'll be less than pleased, I'm sure. But, she can hardly lecture me about morality after what she's done."

"The demons in the theater?"

Lucifer nodded.

"One of my spies told me about that," she said. "I have to say, I was impressed."

"To be honest, so was I. I didn't think this version of my sister had it in her. Human emotions and the like. Well, I should go face the music, I suppose."

"Have fun getting your ass kicked," Allydia called as he scurried down the side of the building.

"I always do," he joked back.

"I remember."

Gabriel met Lucifer at the door. She waited for him to lock it back then grabbed him by the collar and dragged him down the hall to his bedroom.

"What was that about?" Wyatt asked.

"Looks like boss lady's about to whoop some ass," Valerie answered.

Gabriel closed the door behind them and telekinetically threw him across the room, slamming him hard against the wall above his bed.

"The fuck?!" she demanded.

"Come now," he said. "They had it coming."

"I'm not saying I don't understand the impulse, but that is *not* appropriate behavior," she spat. "You can't just go around killing every asshole that deserves a beatdown."

"Why ever not?"

"Because there'd be no people left," she explained. "You got pissed off at the awful things those pricks were saying. Imagine hearing the depraved shit everyone's thinking all the time. If I killed every dumpster-fire human that I deemed unfit to live, the population would plummet by like,--"

"Fifty?" he poked.

She sighed. "I was gonna say 'half', but I take your point. I'm not perfect, either. But--"

"They were brutish degenerates that were abusing their families," he interrupted. "The way I see it, I did the world a favor by removing their wretched chauvinism from the Earth, and in spectacular fashion, if I do say so myself."

"Are you just *too* fucked up?" she wondered. "Did I make a mistake? Should I have left you in a coma? Should I put you back in one?"

"Now, now, don't be cross," he urged. "We haven't much time before Lilith's healed. We should be searching."

"*We've been searching.* While you were off on a murder spree, we've been scouring the city. But, she's still out there, so fine. But, I swear to God, Lucifer, if you pull another stunt like that--"

"You'll what?" he asked, willing himself free and setting his feet on the bed. He stepped down to the floor and walked toward her. "Honestly. You know that I'm the only hope you have of caging our venomous sister and you're keenly aware that if you attempt to go up against her without me, you'll get yourself, not to mention our weaker siblings, killed or worse. She's stronger than you. Stronger than *all of you together*. You *need* me."

"Just because you're *right* doesn't mean you're not a *severe* pain in my ass."

He smirked. "I would apologize for my behavior if I were at all remorseful," he told her.

"As long as you understand why I'm pissed."

"I understand, but it's not as if you didn't know who I was. Now, why don't we move past tonight and focus on the job at hand? We have a monster to capture," he said, walking by her toward the door.

"Lucifer," she said, turning to look at him as he opened the door. He turned to face her again.

"Yes, Gabriel?"

She approached him and, without a word, punched him in the face, breaking his nose and knocking him to the floor. She stepped over him to leave the room as he healed himself.

"I deserved that," he muttered to himself.

"And I already know about crazy-eyes across the street," she called back to him as she walked down the hall.

Chapter 23

Allydia entered her penthouse and was stunned at what she found. Tobin, her Governor of New York, was lying dead in a pool of blood on her foyer floor, his intestines pulled out and strewn around him. She slowly crept down the hall, passing his heart mounted to the wall on a hook that had previously held a mirror, now broken, and his liver and kidneys on the floor among the shards of glass. As she walked into the living room, she saw his lungs lying haphazardly on the coffee table.

"He was one of my favorites," she said when she spotted Lilith clutching her stomach on her chaise. She looked pale and smelled of blood and burned flesh and Allydia wondered what weapon could have rendered her so weak and how she could get her hands on it.

"You shouldn't have had him spying on me, then, daughter," Lilith reprimanded.

"I had to be sure it was you," Allydia explained. "It's been a very long time."

"What is it they say now?" Lilith asked. "Bullshit? Yeah, I'm calling bullshit. And, since when do you lie?"

"Step-Mother, you don't understand,"

"I think I do. You're angry with me because you know what I did in Eridu. That's valid. Had you come to me with your grievances, we could have hashed it out. I may have even apologized. Probably not, but it might have been a possibility. But, you sought out the *angels* for help in getting your revenge, and I can't abide that."

She flicked her wrist, causing a large shard of broken mirror to fly up and plunge into Allydia's back. She gasped, then cried out in pain, reaching behind her to pull it out.

"Don't worry," Lilith told her. "I won't kill you. As disappointed as I am in you and your lack of decision-making skills, I'm hopeful that we can rebuild our relationship. We used to be such a good team, you and I. Do you remember? I miss those days. And the nights! The men and the blood. The *sex*. We can have it all again. Once I'm rid of the angel menace, you'll be by my side, aiding me in reshaping this hopeless planet into the kind of world we deserve. A place where we're worshiped and revered, as I once was before my Father so brutally thrust me into the darkness."

She waved her hand, bending Allydia's spine backward until it snapped. She screamed, falling on the floor in a heap. "Relax," she condescended. "You'll heal in a few minutes. I just want you to *really get* how angry you've made me."

As she lay there, Allydia got a glimpse at her step-mother's abdomen. She had a wound that looked charred at the center with dark lines spreading out from it and blood still slowly trickling out.

"What's wrong with you?" she asked, hoping that distracting her with a new conversation would end the torture.

Lilith looked down at herself and sighed. "This?" she asked, pointing to her stomach. "One of your new friends stuck me with Holy Fire." She waved her hand again, bringing a bookcase crashing down onto the vampire. "I should be fully healed in a few hours. If any of them still live by that time, I'll be able to handle them easily. But, I don't expect to have to."

"I won't kill them," Allydia asserted from under the mess.

"Of course not!" Lilith laughed. "You don't have that kind of power!"

Allydia crawled out from the rubble. "What did you do?"

"Well, they didn't kill *all* of my warriors," she explained. "I know you've been infatuated with one of the angels and I know where they are, thanks to your preoccupation with him."

"Lilith," Allydia warned. "You *can't*."

"I *can't*? You are familiar with me, yes? I can do just about *anything* and I *do not* take orders from *you*. Besides, the demons should be there already, so learn to live with it."

Allydia tried to run for the door, but Lilith threw her to the ground and pulled her back into the living room, never getting up from her seat.

"Can you explain this to me?" she asked. "How is this man your type? Assuming he's roughly the same age as the human Uriel's in, he can't be more than what? Thirty-five? As I recall, older men suited you better. Or, is it that he's *really* several millennia old? Is that what does it for you? That he's ancient?"

The vampire's anger grew, the rage overpowering her common sense. She rushed toward Lilith who smacked her back with her mind like it was nothing.

"An *angel*," Lilith winced. "I thought you had better taste. No matter. He and the others will be gone soon enough and you'll realize that working *with* me instead of against is the right thing to do. We'll have these humans on their knees in a matter of weeks, especially now that you have an entire army of vampires at your command."

"I won't help you," Allydia declared, fighting to stand up again.

"Of course you will," Lilith scoffed. "What is the alternative?"

"I would rather *die* than be your bitch."

"Don't be ridiculous. We'll be partners. Well, seventy/thirty."

"I may not be able to kill you," Allydia said. "But, I will do my damnedest to *fuck you up*."

She lunged for Lilith again, who let out a loud sigh of derision. "Just take your punishment like an adult," she said, flicking her wrist to send Allydia flying through the room and out the window, smashing the glass with her head. She fell, hitting the pavement twelve stories below.

A woman screamed and Allydia could fuzzily see people around her as she struggled to get herself up. As she stood, she was met with a chorus of 'What the hell?'s and 'Holy shit!'s.

"Are you okay?!" someone yelled.

"I'm fine," she told the stranger, her sight restored.

She took her phone from her pocket, but it was crushed. She limped off, hobbling as quickly as she could, hoping she'd be able to warn Wyatt before it was too late.

"We're out of time. We need to get this bitch while she's weak or she'll take off to who knows where and we might never find her," Gabriel told her siblings. The four of them were gathered around the kitchen island, looking over a map of the city. Nervous energy filled the room as everyone was sure *this* would be the night.

"We know she was here," Gabriel said, pointing to the spot on the map where the clinic was located. "We've searched all over Manhattan. She's either left the island, or she's hiding somewhere we wouldn't think to look. At this point, thanks to someone's little adventure," she shot Lucifer an annoyed glance. He smirked. "She could be almost anywhere. I'm guessing she has about three hours before she's one hundred percent, so we need to figure this out and move our asses or we might lose our chance."

"Perhaps, Barachiel could entice his girlfriend to be more helpful in aiding in our efforts," Lucifer mused. "After all, she would most likely do anything he asked her to."

"Asshole," Wyatt muttered.

"That's not a bad idea," Gabriel said. "Dia was supposed to be our Trojan horse, but she's been completely useless so far. Maybe you could give her a call? See if she's been in contact?"

"Or, *you* could call her," Valerie chimed in. "You're the one that brought her into this, to begin with."

"Sure," Gabriel said. "But she's not in love with *me*."

"I don't think 'love' is the right word," Wyatt said.

"Okay," she clarified. "Psychotically obsessed with, then. Either way, you should call her. If she knows something, she's more likely to tell you than anyone. Have you ever read a book or seen a movie where the monster kills everyone and thinks people are garbage, but it has like, a pet? *You're* the pet."

Lucifer snickered.

"That's really condescending," Wyatt told her.

"I'm just being honest with you," Gabriel said. "You're like the bunny that got petted too much so now you have a bald spot. Or the cat that got hugged too hard and your ribs got broken."

Lucifer laughed harder, wiping a tear from his eye.

"Basically," Gabriel continued. "I'm saying the bitch be cray, but you can use that lunacy to maybe help us out."

"Fine," Wyatt agreed. "You'll have to give me her number."

"You don't have her number?" Valerie judged. "Aren't you fuckin' her?"

"Are you giving me shit, too?" he asked.

She threw her hands up and looked away.

He handed Gabriel his phone. She put the number in and handed it back. He put it to his ear, then ended the call and put it back in his pocket.

"Straight to voicemail," he told them.

"She doesn't recognize the number," Valerie assumed.

"That's not the problem," Gabriel said, her eyes darting to the door. "Get ready," she warned.

"Get ready for what?" Valerie asked.

Lucifer felt them now, too. "Demons," he answered, turning to face the door and bracing himself.

Just then, the door flew open, having been kicked in by one of the twelve men that came rushing through, all of them looking pale and sickly.

"Baneful scum," Lucifer vexed. The four stood as the demons rapidly advanced.

Valerie quickly grabbed a butcher's knife from the block on the counter and it instantly burst into flame. She stepped back, hoping to avoid the majority of the fighting while Gabriel began tossing the hellions around the apartment like rag dolls. Wyatt threw lightning at them as they approached, knocking them back hard as Lucifer started to exorcise them one by one.

"I just had this place redone!" Gabriel snapped, sending a demon flying into a wall.

As the others fought, Valerie was surrounded by three lumbering demons. They cackled madly as they closed in, taking twisted pleasure in the terror on her face. She made a futile attempt to stab one of them, but he knocked the blade from her hand, the fire extinguishing upon hitting the wood floor.

"Lilith is most angry with you," the demon hissed.

"Why isn't she here then?" Valerie lashed out. "Cuz she's a scared little bitch, that's why."

The demon growled as he threw his first punch, hitting her in the jaw and knocking her to the floor. The three cheered and laughed as they beat her savagely, punching her face and kicking her in the ribs, back, and head. Once she was motionless, the leader put his hand up for the others to stop and picked up the knife. He used it to brush the hair off her face so he could look into her now glazed-over eyes.

"You're lucky my orders are only to kill you," he wheezed, grasping her by the hair, pulling her head back, and slitting her throat. Blood poured and spurted from the gash as the life drained from Valerie's face. She fell limp to the floor while the three demons howled.

"Valerie!" Gabriel screamed, throwing demons out of her way as she raced to her sister's side. She dropped to her knees, immediately covering the wound on Valerie's neck with one hand and placing the other over her heart. Her hands glowed, white light seeping from the corners of the dead woman's mouth. "Wake up!" Gabriel cried. "I mean it, get your ass up!"

Gradually, the wound healed, and Valerie shot up, gasping for air. She tried to choke out a warning to Gabriel of the demon that was coming up behind her. Just as he raised the knife to stab Gabriel in the back, Wyatt launched a ball of lightning at him, striking him down and rendering him unconscious. Saving his sister, though, meant that Wyatt didn't notice the demon behind *him*, and now, suddenly, there was a cord wrapped around his neck and he was choking.

Before Gabriel could save her brother, another demon grabbed her by the hair and dragged her to the sofa where he began punching her in the face. Valerie hurried to her aid, picking up the knife as she went, leaving Wyatt to handle his attacker on his own. He grabbed the demon's wrists and used all the energy he could to electrocute him, but the supernatural brute was relentless.

Wyatt couldn't breathe, his face turning from red to deep purple as he struggled. The room grew dim and his vision became blurry. As he felt himself beginning to lose consciousness, he heard what sounded like footsteps speeding toward him. Suddenly, he was released, falling on his hands and knees, panting, his chest heaving as he labored to draw breath. He raised up and looked behind him, his vision clearing. He saw Allydia on the back of the demon, viciously tearing his neck apart with her sharp teeth, spewing blood, and flinging tissue everywhere.

Lucifer came to the aid of his sisters, sending the demon they were fighting back to his cage.

When Wyatt's assailant was dead, and the last demon was exorcised, the room went quiet. The human hosts that remained alive were catatonic, having been occupied for so long that their brains were all but destroyed. Gabriel assessed the damage done to her apartment while Valerie sat on a stool at the island, trembling, in near disbelief that she was still alive.

Lucifer paced angrily and Allydia threw up in the sink.

"You all right?" Wyatt asked her.

"Demon blood is highly acidic to things like me," she explained, turning on the faucet and rinsing her mouth out. "I'll be fine."

"You knew about this!" Lucifer accused, grasping Allydia's throat and lifting her off the ground. "I should kill you right now for your treachery."

"Hey!" Wyatt yelled, pushing his brother so hard, he stumbled and dropped the vampire.

"Are you seriously going to defend this creature after what she's done?!" Lucifer barked.

"She wasn't in on it, calm down," Gabriel told him.

"Really?" he asked, not convinced. "How, then, do you explain her sudden appearance only after the object of her affection was put in harm's way?"

Gabriel sighed. "Lilith kicked her ass after figuring out she was helping us, her phone got broken, so she ran over here as fast as she could to warn us," she made clear. "Well, warn *him*, but us by proximity."

"All right, fine," Lucifer conceded, looking Allydia in the eyes. "But, let me be clear. I don't trust you or your motives. Your kind are a plague on this world that, for the life of me, I can't understand why my Father hasn't yet wiped clean from it. If I discover that you assisted my sister in any way, I will rip your head from your body and put your heart in a jar like a trophy on my mantel."

Wyatt stepped between them, staring Lucifer down. "Settle the fuck down," he warned.

Allydia grinned slyly as she stepped away to speak directly to Gabriel. "It will interest you to know that Lilith is at my apartment recovering from whatever one of you did to her. She said it'd be a few hours before she'd be healed, so you can probably still catch her."

"I know," Gabriel told her, having gotten the information as soon as she came in. "I'm just giving these guys a second to get their shit together. Is everybody good?" she asked the others.

"Definitely not good," Valerie admitted.

"Let's go," Gabriel commanded.

As they stepped over bodies to leave, Allydia grabbed Wyatt's arm and he stopped. "Be careful," she warned him. "She's unlike anything you've ever seen. I'm not convinced the four of you can take her."

"I'll be all right," he said, moving her hand gently from his arm. He walked away and when he got to the door, he turned back to look at her for, for all he knew, the last time. "Allydia,"

"Yes," she said, a twinge of excitement flowing through her at the sound of him saying her name.

"Thanks for saving my ass."

"You're more than welcome," she said as he disappeared into the hall. "I'll just clean this up, then!" she called to no one. She looked around the room at the bodies littering the floor, some dead, some barely alive. "What to do with you?"

Chapter 24

The four siblings reached Allydia's apartment, Gabriel blowing the door open with her telekinesis. She and Lucifer began calmly searching through rooms, but Wyatt and Valerie stood motionless in the doorway, horrified by the carnage they saw. Valerie covered her mouth, swallowing a little bit of vomit that had come up in her throat. Wyatt recognized the corpse on the floor from the club and knew Allydia must be upset by the loss. He slowly stepped inside, avoiding slipping on recently removed organs. He made his way to the living room, joining the others. The signs of struggle were evident. The downed bookcase, broken window, and puddles of blood. It was clear to everyone that, had she been human, Allydia would have been killed. It was also clear that she would have been dead, regardless of her species, had Lilith wished it.

"I can feel her," Lucifer said. "She's not far."

"I hear her," Gabriel said, pointing to her temple. "She's on the roof."

They ran up the small flight of stairs that led to Allydia's private rooftop deck and garden. There, they finally found Lilith, sitting on the edge, taking in the view of the city.

"I was sure you'd all be dead by now," she told them, spinning around to face them. "I'd be impressed if I wasn't so irritated." She noticed Valerie, the last to get to the roof, still holding the butcher knife. "Fool me once," she said, shaking her head. She waved her hand in Valerie's direction, throwing her up against the door and wrapping it around her, trapping her in a coffin of metal. She screamed, banging on the door in a desperate attempt to free herself, to no avail.

"Brother," Lilith acknowledged Lucifer, her voice contemptuous.

"Pestiferous obstruction to my well-being," he greeted.

"That's not nice," she replied, holding her hand out. Instantly and with no warning, Lucifer's heart flew from his body and into her awaiting palm. He collapsed in a lifeless heap on the deck.

"Holy shit," Wyatt whispered.

Gabriel was unfazed. "That's a super cute body you've got there," she taunted. "Be a shame if something happened to it." She motioned toward her, engulfing her in flames. She screamed, using unnatural speed to quickly pat out the flames.

"Well, this dress is officially ruined," Lilith said, obviously annoyed. "*And*, you made me drop my new heart. *Gabriel*. You've been a pain in my ass since you were a kindle. Night night." She flicked her wrist, spinning Gabriel's head nearly all the way around, snapping her neck.

"So," she said, turning her attention to Wyatt. "You're the one my daughter's been so taken with." She looked him over, trying to make sense of the vampire's fascination. "I mean, you're *tall*." she conceded. "Are you interesting? Unusually smart or talented? I just don't see it. Not to be insulting, but what *is* it?"

"It's his eyes," Lucifer told her, springing up behind her, grabbing her by the hair and throwing her down onto a snowy patch of soil where, in warmer weather, gardenia's bloomed. "So I'm told." He kicked her hard in the stomach, directly in her mostly-healed wound, reinjuring it enough to put her off her guard for a split second, which was all he needed. He knelt, grabbed his twin's throat with one hand, and plunged the other into her chest. She screeched in agony as he ripped the amulet that kept her planted on the Earth from her body, crushing it to dust.

"How?" Wyatt wondered.

"I'm an archangel, brother," Lucifer explained. "You remove my heart, I'll just grow a new one."

"And I'm pretty quick to snap back myself," Gabriel said, standing up, her spine healed and head back in proper position. She made a fist and stared intently at Lilith, who seemed all but defeated as she coughed up the blood caused by Gabriel crushing her lungs.

Wyatt ran over to Valerie and tried to pry the door open to set her free. Just as he was making a little progress, Gabriel came flying into the wall next to them.

"What the," he started.

"I can't move," she told him.

He turned just as Lilith sent Lucifer flying over the side of the building. Above them, storm clouds gathered in the previously clear sky and the loud crash of thunder filled the air.

"Yo, B!" Gabriel called to him. He met her gaze and she glanced up at the stormy sky and back at him. "You're up." He nodded as Lilith began walking toward him.

"I don't believe we've ever actually met," she said. "You're what, the Protector of Humanity?"

"That's what they tell me."

"Sounds like a burden," she assumed. "No greater burden than what the rest of God's errand boys are tasked with, though, I imagine." She folded her arms and tapped her foot. "What to do, what to do?" she pondered. "Do I kill you so I don't have to look over my shoulder for the next sixty years, or do I spare you, thereby ensuring my daughter's loyalty? Decisions, decisions."

Wyatt quietly gathered all the energy around him, knowing he'd need all he could handle to take her down.

"Answer a question for me," she demanded. "Would it be possible for me to recruit you to my cause? Would you be willing to join me in conquering the human nuisance and ruling over them while waiting on my daughter and I, hand and foot?"

"No," Wyatt answered plainly.

"Pity. 'Protector of Humanity'," she scoffed. "I hate to be the bearer of bad news, but there's nothing you can do to save this world from me."

He gave her a knowing look and a condescending smirk as he raised his hand, rounded up all the energy in the clouds, and brought down a truly massive bolt of lightning. It ripped through the air, brighter than anything human eyes could tolerate and so hot, it melted the snow on the roof before striking Lilith directly on the top of her head, plunging through her, and knocking Wyatt back.

Lilith fell, dazed, her breathing shallow, her eyes glossy. Gabriel was released, her feet barely touching the ground before she used her telekinetic ability to free Valerie.

"Smite!" Gabriel exclaimed giddily.

Wyatt stood and approached Lilith. He raised his hand once more, preparing to strike her again, but before he had the chance, Lucifer appeared behind her, having floated up the side of the building. He knelt behind his twin, placing one hand on her heart and grasping her arm with the other.

"I realize it's been some time since we were last together on Earth," he said to her as the hand on her chest began to glow. "But, did you honestly forget that I can fly?"

Lilith's body shook as if she were having a violent seizure. Blood poured from her nose, mouth, and ears. Even her eyes spilled tears of blood. Lucifer's face remained determined, his eyes watching closely to make sure that after the darkness that was her essence slowly and painfully peeled away from the girl she had been inhabiting, it went back to where it belonged in the deepest and most secure part of Hell.

"See you at home, sister," he whispered as the last bit of her disappeared. "You're welcome," he said, looking up at Wyatt as the skies inexplicably cleared.

"That was you?" Wyatt asked.

"I thought you could use the assist. Now, if you'll excuse me, I need to get this girl to a hospital. Seems the poor dear has suffered a lightning strike." Lucifer grinned, gathered Lilith's ex-host, who remained unconscious, and jumped off the roof, floating down and running with inhuman speed to the nearest emergency room.

"Will she be okay?" Wyatt asked Gabriel.

"Not even close," she told him. "But, she's probably got family looking for her. At least they won't be left wondering if she's dead in a ditch somewhere."

"I guess," he muttered, feeling guilty about hurting the innocent child Lilith had taken hostage.

"Hey," Gabriel consoled. "You did what had to be done to save humankind. And, that poor kid's brain would've been mush no matter how or when Lilith left, just like the demons at home. Speaking of which, we should go figure out what to do with those bodies. I vote dumpster fire. Worked for Lucifer."

"What?" Wyatt asked.

"What?"

"So," Valerie asked. "She's gone? Like, all the way gone? We're done?"

"Totes," Gabriel responded.

"For real?"

"Yeah, bitch is gone."

"Well, shit," Valerie beamed. "I'm gonna go home, smoke a bowl, and relax for the first time in months!" She ran down the stairwell, got in the elevator, and was gone.

Gabriel laughed as she and Wyatt followed down the steps.

"You're not gonna follow Lucifer?" he asked. "You seemed pretty pissed when he went off on his own earlier."

"Nah," Gabriel replied. "I know what he was thinking about and it wasn't wreaking havoc. He met a girl."

"Ah."

"Yeah, a hot bartender chick."

"Nice."

"Like, really hot."

"Okay," Wyatt chuckled.

"I mean, like, *stupid* sexy."

"That's great."

"Slammin' body."

"Do you want to be alone?"

"No, but if I go out later, don't wait up," she instructed.

He laughed as they exited the building and began the walk back to Gabriel's apartment. "I guess I have to go home and pack up my place. I don't want to live there without Annie. It doesn't feel right."

"You know you can stay with me as long as you want," she invited. "Just because we don't have a villain to vanquish doesn't mean we're not still family."

"I appreciate that, but I need to figure my life out," he told her. "I have all this property to deal with, sell off, something. I should check on my dad before I go."

"This all sounds like future problems to me," she declared. "Tomorrow stress. Tonight, I say we watch bad reality TV and drink."

"What is with you and reality shows?" he wondered.

"When people are on TV," she explained. "I don't know what they're thinking. Makes me feel like a normal person. Or, what I think a normal person must feel like. Not knowing what someone's about to say or do. It's exciting. Like a roller coaster."

"Okay," he laughed. "But, can we eat? I'm starving."

"Pizza," she said knowingly.

"Obviously."

Chapter 25

The next day, Wyatt packed his car with the clothes Gabriel had bought him, at her insistence, along with the file of his uncle's properties, and began the sixty-eight-mile drive back to his New Jersey apartment. As he drove, he couldn't get the image of that poor girl out of his mind. Her dead-behind-the-eyes stare as Lucifer stripped Lilith from her haunted him. Who was she? What could she have grown up to be had she not been made Lilith's sacrificial lamb? What could her life have been like? Knowing that it wasn't his fault that she was comatose and that her family was surely devastated by her condition, which he knew to be permanent, didn't help him to feel any less guilty. She was just a kid. It wasn't right. It wasn't fair.

He was almost home, having gotten off I-95 on Garden State Parkway when his phone rang. He took it from his pocket and put it on speaker.

"Hello?"

"Hello," a strange man's voice replied. "May I speak to Wyatt Sinclair?"

"This is Wyatt."

"Mr. Sinclair, this is Dr. Laurence, your wi--"

"You're breaking up," Wyatt told the caller. "Did you say 'my wife'?"

"Yes," the doctor said, speaking louder as if that would somehow give Wyatt better reception. "Annie suf--,"

"She what?" Wyatt asked, his stomach dropping as he tried to focus on the road and make out what the doctor was saying.

Through the garbled, robot-sounding syllables and static, Wyatt could make out a few words: 'Central Medical Center', 'need you', and 'DNR'. His heart sank as the call dropped. 'DNR'. 'Do not resuscitate'. His hands shook and his heart raced. He thought he might hyperventilate as he altered course, speeding to the hospital, ignoring stop signs and traffic lights on the way, almost getting into several accidents, blind to the world around him. Once there, he raced into the building, barely getting the car door closed before he sprinted through the parking lot. He worked to stifle his anxiety as he quickly approached the front desk.

"I'm looking for Annie Sinclair," he told the receptionist.

She typed something in her computer before looking back up at him, concern in her eyes. "Second floor," she said quietly. "Room two-sixteen. But--"

"Thank you," he called as he ran to the elevator, frantically pressing the up button. It opened immediately and he stepped inside. As the doors closed, he took a few deep breaths and tried to calm himself.

When the doors opened again, he searched the room numbers along the hall. 208, 210, 212.

"Can I help you, sir?" a chipper nurse asked.

"I'm just looking for room 216," he told her.

Her face fell. "Are you Mr. Sinclair?" she questioned, her voice shaky.

"Yes."

"Wait right here," she instructed. "I'll get the doctor." She hurried back to the nurse's station and he watched as she made a call, the two other nurses there shooting him sympathetic glances. He knew it was bad. He again checked room numbers. 214 and, finally, 216. As he reached for the handle, a man in a white coat put his hand on his shoulder, gently turning Wyatt to face him.

"Mr. Sinclair, I'm Dr. Laurence," he said, removing his hand from Wyatt's shoulder. He reached out to shake Wyatt's hand, but Wyatt ignored it. "Mr. Sinclair," he continued, ignoring the snub. "I'm very sorry. We did everything we could, but--"

"But, what?" Wyatt asked, his voice raised.

The doctor was visibly uncomfortable but worked to maintain his composure. "I'm sorry," he said again. "I'll give you a few minutes to say goodbye before she's moved."

"Moved where?" Wyatt seethed.

"Mr. Sinclair, your wife made it very clear that in these circumstances, she wanted her viable organs harvested for donation. I know it sounds grim, but it's actually--"

"What circumstances?"

"Well, brain death, sir."

Wyatt was crushed. Tears filled his eyes as he felt the world come crashing down around him. He opened the door to the room and what he saw broke him. She was there, lying in the hospital bed, hooked up to tubes and wires, machines beeping all around her. He felt his legs go weak and he thought he might pass out.

"Take your time," the doctor said, closing the door, leaving Wyatt alone.

His heart pounded in his ears as he drew closer. How could this be happening? She was only thirty-five. He stood over her, touching her soft, blond hair, the sight of her chest rising and falling with such force breaking his heart even more.

He fell to his knees, sobbing, touching her face and burying his own in the pillow next to hers, the smell of her lavender shampoo filling his lungs. He screamed into the pillow, the sorrow overwhelming him. He had never felt such pain, the anguish taking him over completely. As he wailed, the lights in the room began to flicker. One of the bulbs in the overhead light blew out, shaking Wyatt free of his misery. *Of course.* His wife may have been technically dead, but she didn't necessarily have to stay that way.

Gabriel, he thought. *I need you. I need you right now.*

On my way, she responded.

"It's okay, baby," he said to the body, wiping the tears from his face. "We're gonna fix this. You'll be all right."

He sat in a chair next to the bed, holding the corpse's hand for over an hour as he impatiently waited, his leg shaking and his mind racing. Finally, Gabriel showed up, hurrying into the room, ignoring the nurses that tried to stop her.

"Jesus, B. I'm so sorry," she said, putting her hand on his shoulder. "What do you need?"

"I need you to wake her up."

"I don't think--"

"You did it for Lucifer," he reminded. "You did it for Valerie."

"Lucifer wasn't," she paused, trying to be tactful. "*This.* He was just stuck. And, Valerie would've been fine on her own, I just overreacted in the moment. I don't know if I can help here."

"Tae told me you could raise the dead. He *told me.* I've seen you. You can do *anything.* Please," he begged. "*Please.*"

"Okay, I'll try," she agreed, feeling his desperation. She went around to the other side of the bed and placed one hand on the dead woman's head and the other on her heart. Gabriel's hands glowed, but Annie's skin did not. After a few minutes, she gave up.

"I can't," she said softly, coming back around to stand in front of her brother. "Her soul's already gone."

"Then bring it back!" he commanded, jolting up from his seat.

"The Gates are closed. Only human souls can get in. I'm locked out."

"Do *something!*" he shouted, grabbing his sister's shoulders.

"Wyatt!" she said, her use of his human name jarring him into silence. He let her go and steadied his breath. "I'm really sorry, but your girl's gone."

He collapsed back in the chair, tears again streaming down his face. Gabriel knelt in front of him and took his hands in hers.

"Listen," she said. "I know, coming from a normal person, that saying, 'she's in a better place' would be cliche' and not comforting whatsoever. But, you can believe me when I tell you, Heaven is fan-fucking-tastic. I can guarantee you, she's happy as shit up there right now."

He wiped his tears away and tried to get it together. He looked over at his wife and stroked her hair one last time.

"It's not fair," he uttered. "We weren't together, but she was still--"

"No," Gabriel said, standing back up. "It's not fair. It's kind of bullshit. But, at least you don't have to think about her banging some other dude anymore."

"That's *really* not helpful."

A knock came from the door and it opened just enough for a nurse to poke her head in.

"He's all ready to go," she told them before quickly disappearing back into the hall.

Wyatt stood and started toward the door, giving his wife one final glance.

"What the," Gabriel whispered.

"She donated her organs," he told her. "The doctor's been waiting."

"That's not..." Her voice trailed off as they left the room, Wyatt stopping in the hall to look back inside, the space now filled with medical personnel blocking his view of Annie's face. He brushed away one last tear as he resigned himself to the fact that she was really gone.

"Here we are," the nurse said from behind him. He turned to see her standing beside a cart with bags on the bottom and a car seat on top. Strapped into the seat was a tiny baby covered by a striped blanket.

"I'm sorry, what?" he asked, profoundly confused.

"He's had all of his tests, his vitamin K and Hep B shots," she explained. "All the follow-up information is in the folder in the bag along with his diapers, wipes, and a few bottles of the formula he's been on. He's a very good eater, aren't you?" she said playfully, booping the infant's nose. "Oh! Almost forgot. Let me just get the scissors to take off his bracelet and you can be on your way." She walked off, disappearing into one of the rooms.

Wyatt walked closer to the cart, standing over the baby who looked up at him and cooed. He lifted the blanket and examined the bracelet around the child's ankle. It had Annie's name and the day before's date typed on it.

"Angel of Blessings," Gabriel muttered shakily.

"I don't understand," he said quietly. "She was having an affair for *months* before she left? That's--"

"Not what happened," Gabriel told him.

He looked at his sister who, for the first time since he'd met her, looked nervous. More than nervous. She looked downright scared.

"You're telling me he's *mine*?" Wyatt asked, disbelief coloring his voice. "I thought there was no way."

"He has your eyes," she said, her voice trembling.

He looked back down at the newborn and realized she was right. He looked *just* like Wyatt's baby pictures. "How?" he asked, a quiver now in his voice, as well.

Gabriel glanced around quickly to make sure no one was in earshot. "Lightning isn't your only thing," she explained. "Barachiel is also the Angel of Blessings. Sometimes, when a woman prays for a baby, you make sure she gets one. I didn't think you could do that in this form. It requires a metric fuckton of power. But, she must have prayed to get knocked up while you two were boning and you unknowingly answered that prayer," she told him. "With your dick."

The nurse returned with the scissors and carefully cut the bracelet from the baby's ankle. "There you go, William," she said. "That's got to be more comfortable, huh?"

"Did you say, 'William'?" Wyatt asked.

"Yes," she said happily. "Oh, had you not settled on a name before?" she asked, realizing the situation. "I hope it's all right. She told the doctor his name should be William Ross Sinclair."

"It's fine," he said, his voice weak.

The nurse rubbed his arm in a pitiful attempt at comforting him while still remaining peppy. "Well, he's perfectly healthy," she said. "Congratulations." And with that, she was gone, scurrying into another room with another patient.

The siblings awkwardly made their way to the elevator, Wyatt carrying the baby in the car seat and Gabriel taking the bags.

"She named him William," Wyatt said, still in shock.

"Yeah."

"That's my middle name," he said as they boarded the elevator, the doors closing slowly behind them.

"I know."

"Ross was her dad's name. He died when we were in college. She always said if we ever had a kid, she'd want to name it after him. But, she put *my* name *first*."

"Mm-hmm."

"Don't you get it?" he asked, a small bit of happiness breaking through the waves of despair. "She never had a *boyfriend. He* was the other guy! She left me because she was worried I'd hurt him in a schizophrenic fit. She didn't stop loving me," he realized, looking down at his child in amazement. "She just loved him more."

The doors opened and they left the hospital, passing the concerned-looking receptionist as they went. Once at the car, Wyatt struggled with the car seat as Gabriel put the bags in the trunk on top of her brother's suitcases. She saw the file sticking out from underneath everything else and picked it up before closing the trunk and walking around to where Wyatt stood, finally having secured the baby in the back seat.

"I can't see him," she admitted.

"What do you mean?" Wyatt asked. "He's right there."

"I can *see* him, with my eyes. But, I can't *see* him, inside. I can't hear his thoughts or see his memories. I don't know what he's feeling. It's like he's not there."

"What are you talking about?" he questioned, suddenly feeling defensive and intensely protective of his new son. "What are you saying to me right now?"

"You know--"

"What?!"

"Barachiel," she said sternly. "He's Nephilim."

"No," he said firmly, closing the car door and standing between it and his sister. "Gabriel, don't even think it."

"I should kill him," she told him. "Now, before things get ugly."

Wyatt formed a ball of lightning and stared at her fiercely.

"If I was gonna do it, you wouldn't be able to stop me," she said. "But, I'm not going to, *against* my better judgement. But, Lucifer *will*. If he finds out there's a Nephilim on Earth, he *will* take him out."

Wyatt extinguished the lightning but didn't yet relax.

"I won't tell him," she promised. "Or Valerie. But, you have to go." She thrust the file with his uncle's property listings in it into his hand. "Take him somewhere *far*. Way away from people. He's gonna grow stupid fast and when he's done, he'll get his powers. He won't be able to handle them."

"I'll teach him."

"You'll try," she said. "You'll do everything you can to turn him into a decent person, but--"

"He'll be fine," Wyatt insisted.

"He'll be fucked the fuck up," she warned. "He'll get crazier and more violent and, eventually, he'll go completely off the rails."

"I can deal with it."

"If you can't," she urged. "If and when he gets too dangerous and you need help, *you call me*." She pointed to her temple.

He nodded.

She sighed, unsure of her decision. She threw her arms around Wyatt's neck and hugged him tightly, worried about what raising this monstrosity would do to him, but knowing that if she did what her instincts were telling her to, he'd never forgive her.

"I love you, you big, stupid crybaby," she told him.

He chuckled. "Love you, too."

"All right," she said, backing away. "I'll take care of your place, have your stuff shipped to wherever. Now, get out of here before I change my mind."

She didn't have to tell him twice. He hurried around the car to the driver's side door, opened it, and got in. "Thank you!" he called before slamming it shut.

"Don't make me regret it!" she called back as he sped away. "I already do," she said to herself. She sighed again, watching them drive off, her brother having no real idea of what he was getting himself into. She cracked her neck and groaned, "Fuck my life."

Wyatt made his way to I-276 and glanced up in the mirror at his new son who sat calmly in the backseat, the sweetest baby he'd ever seen. "Don't worry, Will," he said. "We're gonna be fine."

He checked the map on his phone to make sure he was going the right way. "Looks like we're moving to Indiana."

Chapter 26

Michelle tossed her diploma and cap on the sofa before collapsing onto it herself. She flopped her feet up on the ottoman and picked up the remote. While her classmates were off at their respective receptions and open houses, gathering gifts and 'congratulations', she was alone, watching TV and trying not to dwell on the fact that she had no family to celebrate her; no one to be proud of her.

The last four months since her uncle died had been tough. She barely made it through school and her social life was basically non-existent. She had isolated herself, for the most part, in the apartment Tae had left her, her only consolation being that, since he'd left her everything in his will, she didn't have to fret about college, work, or money. She was taken care of, and no matter what she decided to do with her life, she'd be okay, financially speaking. Emotionally, however, she was barely holding it together. Everyone she'd ever cared about or counted on was gone. She was sullen and resentful, jealous of the kids in her class that looked so happy after the commencement, posing for pictures and hugging their parents. It had taken everything she had to hold back the tears until she was safely in a cab and on her way home, away from the judgemental eyes of her classmates and the feigned sympathy of the parents and school staff. No one in that place had ever actually cared about her. She was friendly with a few of the kids, but there was no one there she'd really consider a true friend and no boys had ever taken any interest in her. The teachers were fine, but the administration was blatantly racist, whispering slurs when they thought she couldn't hear while parading her around during fundraisers and tours to show how 'diverse' the campus was. When her uncle died, Michelle almost dropped out, partly due to grief, but also out of spite. She knew they'd need her to be present at their mid-year open house and she so badly wanted to show up there with a bullhorn, give a brutal speech about how bigoted the Headmaster and her cronies were, and burn the whole place to the ground. She didn't, of course, because no matter how awful the people in that school were, a diploma from there was a guaranteed ticket to any college she wanted to attend, and more importantly, she knew how important it had been to Tae that she get a good education. So, she sucked it up, did what she had to, and graduated third in her class.

She glanced over at the dining table on the other side of the room, the pile of thick envelopes from all six universities she applied to sitting in the middle of it like a demanding centerpiece, mocking her indecision. She knew she had very little time to choose one, but the thought of going to college in the fall was overwhelming. Just the idea of opening the acceptance letters was stressful to the point of panic, and the longer she procrastinated, the worse her anxiety got. She looked back at the television and decided to put it off for another day. After all, she just graduated from high school. She'd earned a little relaxation time.

There was a knock at the door, which was odd since no one had been to visit in months. She turned off the TV, got up, and opened the door.

"Cute outfit," the woman in the hall said, referencing the gown Michelle had been too lazy to take off.

"Can I help you?" she asked.

"You can let me in," the woman told her. "Your uncle never gave my 'Sixteen Stone' CD back. I let him borrow it like, twenty years ago, thinking it'd open him up to different kinds of music than what he was used to. Classical and opera. I mean, I like a good Renaissance piece as much as the next girl, but come on. *All the time?* Snooze. I let him keep it because he kind of had a thing for the singer, but I mean, who didn't, right? Anyways, if I could get that back, that'd be awesome."

"I'm sorry," Michelle said suspiciously. "Who are you?"

The woman smiled. "Gabriel. Tae told you about me. He wasn't *supposed* to, but what are you gonna do?"

"You're," the girl breathed. "The Messenger of--"

"That's me. Now, can you let me in? We need to talk."

"Of course!" Michelle agreed, stepping out of the way to let the angel through. She stepped inside.

"I'm serious about that CD," Gabriel told her as the door closed behind her.

The End

The Complete Seventh Day Series

Seraphim
Nephilim
Elohim
Cain
Alukah
Coven
Sinclair

Made in the USA
Las Vegas, NV
06 October 2021

31832181R00121